DARK OFFERING

Elizabeth James

Thrall of Darkness

Dark Offering was published serially on thrallofdarkness.com in 2019.

CONTENTS

CHAPTER 1

The sun glimmered on the metallic spires of the colony, starting its slow rise into the sky. Jarl glanced up briefly, but the splendor of the scene was lost on him. The days were short this time of year, though they were starting to get longer, but tonight, nightfall would hold no danger. Normally, the darkness unleashed the hidden creatures of the night who devoured any humans foolish enough to wander about. For a brief time in the spring, however, the creatures were docile. It was as though the planet were trying to apologize for its harshness, and it was a glimpse of what life could be like if the planet would only accept humans into its ecosystem.

It wasn't the humans' fault that the planet rejected them, Jarl thought bitterly. When human colonists had first found the planet, they had thought it a second Earth. They had left their home planet seeking a place to grow without making the mistakes that had led to the destruction of original Earth, and they thought they had found it here. And the truth wasn't apparent for some time, because at first the native creatures stayed away. So the colonists broke their landing ship into components to build their housing, and soon the ability to leave the surface was lost. It was then that they realized the planet was just waiting to strike.

Jarl sighed. This sweet peace in the spring held so much promise. The original colonists had thought it would always be like this, but now, people knew better. In a few short days, the nights would once again hold terror as anything with human consciousness became warped by nightmares that led humans straight into the mouths of the creatures outside.

He was headed into the wilderness for the annual harvest which took advantage of the planet's brief peace. There were plants deep in the woods of Ylse that provided the perfect nutritional balance for humans and remained fresh for years, and because it was so difficult growing anything in the protected colony where humans were trapped, they were a vital supplement to the colony's diet. This was the only time of year when it was safe enough to travel into the woods to gather them, and he had been doing it for three years now. The old timers said they sometimes ran into the creatures of the planet during these harvests, but Jarl never had. The planet left him alone, as it left all humans alone during this single moment in the spring.

It had to do with the moon, Jarl knew. Something about how it neutralized the waves that filtered into human consciousness. He wasn't sure, but he was grateful. He hefted his empty bags and adjusted his mask. It was said that once a creature saw your face, they could haunt your dreams until you willingly went to your death as the siren's wail of the planet's odd emanations manipulated your desires.

By the time the sun sank, the colony was out of sight and he was surrounded by the woods. There were no humans within miles of him and he shivered in fear. Even though he knew he was safe, it was unnerving being outside of the colony's protection as it grew dark and the sun slipped below the treeline.

Every time he did this, he was amazed at the silence of the night. Normally, there was a low hum that translated into nightmares. When the nightmares were too strong, they manifested into action as the person tried to leave the colony and go to their death. Guards were stationed at every exit to protect people, but there were still casualties almost every night. On Earth, nightmares were passive, he knew. They were frightening, but couldn't kill you. He envied the original colonists their innocence, and he envied the people of original Earth for the ability to sleep without fear. He had heard it was even possible to sleep without nightmares, though the concept was utterly alien to him. Even when he slept during the day, there were nightmares. They just weren't strong enough to kill.

When his legs started to tire, he came to a stop. It was nearly pitch black but he could see clearly with his night vision goggles that sat above his mask. The silence was unnerving as he considered resting. It was important to get to the plants quickly and return before the planet roared back to life, but he would need to rest eventually. He had five days to get there and back, and while he needed to rush, he shouldn't push himself past his limits. He looked around. This was a good place to rest. The trees were a little farther apart and the undergrowth formed a protective barrier where he could sleep. Yes, he would take a rest here. He knelt in the hollow on the ground and heard a sound behind him.

Jarl drew in a sharp breath and whirled, whipping up his gun even though he knew the weapon wouldn't help him against most creatures that came out at night. The power of the moon helped them heal too quickly. Only in the daylight could they be killed, and they had long ago learned that and hid when the sunlight's rays weakened them.

There was nothing. Nothing behind him, only the trees. He ought to be able to see any heat nearby but nothing was showing up. He scanned the area completely. Maybe he had misheard it, or maybe it was just a natural sound of the woods that was exaggerated in the silence of the spring night.

He cautiously knelt on the ground and looked around again, and then lay down. He curled up protectively and fell into sleep, his mind swirling into nightmares of sharp teeth piercing his veins and wispy shapes draining him of life. A peaceful sleep, compared to most, and when he awoke he felt rested. It was still dark as he got to his feet and looked around. The sun was about to rise and he needed to keep going. Four days left.

CHAPTER 2

The day went well, and as night started to fall again, he knew that if he pushed, he could reach the plants before he rested. He would get there, sleep, then collect the plants in the morning and start heading back. The plants grew in specific locations that the original colonists had mapped out carefully and the paths to them were well-known to the harvesters like Jarl. There were twelve patches where they grew within range of the colony and one harvester had set out for each one. Jarl's patch was the farthest, but he had made good time.

The woods were mostly silent during the day, but he kept hearing an unusual clopping sound. Every time he heard it, he looked around and saw nothing out of place. The creatures of the day were harmless but a few were curious about humans and sometimes followed them, so he assumed that was the sound. As the sun sank into the sky again and he put his night goggles on, he scanned the area. There were scattered patches of heat as the day creatures sank into their cold sleep and grew nearly invisible, and soon it was only him again. Only tonight, the silence was broken by the sound of wind.

Jarl shivered every time the wind picked up, waiting for it to infiltrate his mind and lead him to death. His pace quickened. But nothing happened. His nerves were fraying, but he was safe. He tried to assure himself of that over and over again. He was safe. The planet didn't kill during this single peace. He was safe.

He came to the crest of a small hill and looked down into the valley below. The plants were straight ahead and he let out a sigh of relief. He had made it. He took off his night goggles as the plants were phosphorescent and lit the area with a warm glow. He headed into the final stretch with a light heart and when he saw the dense foliage start to give way to the clearing where the enormous pod-like plants sprouted, the tension drained from his shoulders. Not even the wind bothered him. He grinned as he reached the first of the shoulder-height bloom, but when he stepped into the clearing, his smile slipped. Ice shot through his spine and his heart skidded into a frantic tattoo as his fight-or-flight instincts consumed him. A creature stood there, and it wasn't human.

Jarl dropped into a crouch and pointed his gun at the humanoid shape. He had never seen a creature of the night and was a little surprised at how human it looked. And it made no moves towards him, though it was looking at him. His hands trembled with adrenaline as he struggled to figure out what to do. If it were any other time of year, he would be dead right now. The creatures could move faster than humans and he wouldn't stand a chance. But he was safe, and other humans had met these creatures during this brief period of safety and survived.

He took a deep breath. Shooting the creature would do nothing and there was no point in running. He would stand his ground and hope that the creature left. In the meantime, he studied it curiously.

It was human in form, and while it seemed to wear draping clothing of some sort, it appeared to be male. He wasn't entirely human, but he was more beautiful than anything Jarl could have imagined. He was nearly a head taller than Jarl and his muscular body showed clearly under the cloth. His skin had a lovely bronze tint, as if he spent all his time in the sun, but his fingers seemed unnaturally long. He had a square jaw and strong nose, but his eyes were larger than they should be and entirely black, like an insect's eyes. Still, he was lovely to look at and Jarl was startled that a creature of the night could be so beautiful. His hands were angled up as if to indicate peace. Or at least Jarl hoped it indicated peace. Then the creature smiled, exposing a full mouth of razor sharp fangs, and Jarl stepped back nervously. Every one of the creature's teeth were at least two inches long and came to a severe point, curving slightly inward in a mockery of a smile.

"I mean you no harm," the creature said in perfect English. "Put down your gun."

Jarl lowered his gun, because he knew his gun was useless anyway.

"My name is Arlen. What is yours?"

Jarl licked his lips. He had never heard of a creature talking to a human before. They ate humans, not conversed with them. He wracked his brain for what the old timers had said about these encounters, but it seemed like they only glimpsed the creatures. He had never heard of anyone coming face to face with a creature like this and surviving. But the creature showed no animosity or aggression. If anything, the creature looked quite curious. And the smile, though threatening given his fangs, might be meant to reassure. But he remembered that once a creature saw your face, it could drag you to your death. His mask was still securely in place and he had to assume hearing a human's voice had the same weakness. He would stay silent. The creature's smile faded.

"I mean you no harm," he repeated. "You've come for these plants, haven't you? I won't stop you."

Jarl looked around, wondering if the creature would stay here while he harvested the plants. Would the creature stay until he left? He had been planning on sleeping here, but there was no way he could sleep with this thing nearby.

Cautiously, he went to the first plant and ran his hand over the petals to spark the stamen to extend. It obeyed and he was aware of the creature watching him with that same curiosity. Carefully, Jarl harvested the pollen pods that provided much-needed nutrients and packed them into his bags. He took a bite of one to make sure it was ripe to eat and the honey-sweet taste flooded his senses as he couldn't hold back a sigh of pleasure. Not only were the plants nutritious, they were absolutely delicious.

He harvested the first plant completely and looked at the nearest plant. The creature was between him and the plant. He wasn't going to get any closer, but he needed the pollen. The creature smiled again.

"Aren't you curious why such a perfect plant exists?" he asked. Jarl's eyes narrowed. "It wasn't here before you humans arrived. Aren't you curious about it?"

Jarl was tempted to say the plant must have been here before, since plants couldn't have evolved since human arrived over a hundred years ago. Not a plant this large and elaborate. But he wondered at those words, and at the plant itself. It didn't make sense that there was a plant perfectly catered to human needs on such an inhospitable planet.

"Aren't you curious why we give you time to reach the plants every year?"

Jarl hesitated.

"What do you mean?" he asked, then bit his tongue. He had spoken. He braced himself, but there was no siren wail to go to his death. He was safe, for the time being. The creature's smile widened into a grin.

"So you are curious. We're curious, too. About you. Humans. You're alien to us and we've tried to adapt, but your minds are toxic to us. We want to assimilate you, but we can't."

"What are you talking about?"

"Your dreams," the creature said. "Our planet has tried to communicate to you, but you're numb to her. Why can't you hear her? Why does her voice drive you insane?"

"I don't know what you're talking about," Jarl said nervously, not liking the fact that they were talking about the dreams that might lead him to his death when the planet's viciousness returned.

"Do you know why I'm here?"

"No."

"What's your name?"

Jarl edged backwards. Was there some power in knowing his

name? Well, he was likely going to die anyway. The creature had heard his voice. Was there a reason why he should hold back his name?

"Why do you want to know?"

"You're intended for me," the creature said, and Jarl shivered and took several steps backwards. So it was too late. He would be devoured by this creature as soon as the darkness regained its power.

"I hope you survive," the creature added. "We keep hoping for a human to survive. None ever has, but we thought perhaps if we spoke to you first, got to know you a little, you might survive. I've told you my name. It's only fair for you to do the same."

"Jarl," he whispered.

"Pleasure to meet you, Jarl," the creature said, looking pleased.

"When will you kill me? Will you let me bring these plants back to the colony first?"

"If you return before the night regains her power, then you'll be safe," he said. "But once she does, you'll be drawn to me. It's inevitable. They can stop you for a day, maybe a week, but eventually you'll find me. And I hope you survive."

"Why do you want me to survive? Don't you want to feed on me?"

"We want to learn to feed without killing," the creature said. "Wouldn't you prefer that? If humans could live in harmony with our planet? That's all we want."

Jarl considered. He did want humans to live in harmony, but he didn't want them to be fed on. Couldn't the planet just leave them alone? He glanced at the plant behind the creature. The creature moved out of his way as if he knew what Jarl wanted, and gestured to it.

"You should harvest all of them," the creature said. Very warily, Jarl moved to the plant and stroked the petals. He tasted the pollen to make sure it was ripe, then began filling his bag again. When he finished, the creature moved so that he could access another.

"Aren't you tired?" the creature asked as he finished the third plant. He was tired. He had planned on getting here, sleeping, and then harvesting in the morning. But there was no way he was sleeping with this creature around. "You should rest. Your kind aren't used to the nights."

"I'm fine," he said.

The creature took a step towards him and he flinched back. The creature raised his arms as if to indicate that he meant no harm.

"You should rest. If I didn't hurt you last night, I'm not going to tonight."

"You've been following me?" he asked nervously, remembering the sounds he had been hearing. But there had been nothing in his goggles. Nothing alive had been near him.

"Look at me with those goggles," the creature said, gesturing to the night goggles hanging at his neck. Cautiously, he put them on over his mask. And was stunned. There was nothing in front of him. The plants glowed red, but there no creature standing in front of him. It wasn't even that the creature was cold, because otherwise he would see it outlined against the hot plants. There was no trace of him. He lowered the goggles quickly, wondering if the creature had left. He was still there, smiling. A chill went down Jarl's spine. No one had ever suspected that the creatures of the night could hide from their goggles.

"You see?" the creature said. "I won't hurt you. But you should rest before you continue. You'll have plenty of time to harvest the rest of these tomorrow and you'll be able to return with time to spare. You shouldn't push yourself."

"Why should you care? You're just going to eat me when the darkness returns."

"I told you, I want you to survive," the creature said. "You can't survive if you die on the way back. And your people depend on this harvest."

Jarl looked at the plants, then at the ground. He had slept here before when he came to harvest. He had always assumed it was safe. And he did need rest. But how could he possibly rest with a creature like this nearby?

"Would you prefer if I left?" the creature asked. "I won't go far, but perhaps you would prefer privacy."

"Yes," he said, though he wasn't sure he would trust any privacy he got. If he couldn't see the creature, how could he know he had privacy? Normally he slept on the outskirts of this clearing so the light from the plants was dimmer. This time he would have to sleep in the middle of them to feel safe and he didn't now if their light would interfere with his sleep.

"Sleep well, then," the creature said, and headed towards the woods.

Jarl let out a slow breath, stunned by everything that had just happened. He had spoken to a creature of the night. An extended conversation. And his soul had been claimed, he thought with a chill. When this brief peace ended, his nightmares would drive him out of the colony. The creature was right. The guards could stop most people, but every night at least one person managed to get by. Eventually, he would get by and he would be drawn straight to that creature to be devoured. Unless he wasn't, he considered. Unless somehow he survived, as the creature claimed he wanted. It was too confusing to think about and he lay down cautiously. Sleep came slowly, but soon he was caught up in an eery wailing accompanied by flashing fangs, a typical dream, and he managed to rest.

CHAPTER 3

The horizon was just starting to turn crimson when he opened his eyes and stretched. Three days left. Then he remembered what had happened and bolted up, looking around. No one was here and he let out a sigh of relief. Then he saw his mask on the ground in front of him and his heart skidded to a stop. He held out a trembling hand and picked it up, looking around again. He heard a clopping sound and swiftly put the mask on. Had he taken it off in his dreams? Why wasn't it on his face? The creature appeared and he sat up, face protected once more.

"There's no point in wearing that," the creature said, gesturing to the mask.

"You saw me?" he whispered.

"I was curious. You are intended for me, after all. I should know what you look like. And we don't have to see your faces to draw you."

He tensed. "You don't?"

"No," the creature said. "It makes it more likely to happen, but some of you are just drawn to us no matter what you do. You would be drawn to me regardless of whether or not I saw your face, and I was curious."

Jarl shivered. That meant the creature had gotten close enough to take off his mask while he was sleeping. So much for the creature giving him privacy. He never should have trusted him and he would never make that mistake again.

"You humans are quite beautiful," the creature added. "You especially. I'm glad you're intended for me."

"Why does it matter what I look like if you're just going to eat me?" he asked gruffly, getting to his feet and looking around. The creature smiled.

"I want you to survive," he said. "I think you might. But I have to go now. You'll be safe during the day."

The sun was rising and Jarl realized that the creature of course couldn't be here once the sun came up. He would have to do as much as possible while he could. The creature got up and headed into the shadows of the woods and Jarl waited until the sun had broken the horizon before going to the edge of the plants to use the bathroom. Then he got back to harvesting and soon his bags were full. He hefted them over his shoulder. The pollen was light but quite bulky and it always took longer getting back. He had calculated that into his plans, though. This might be the farthest patch, but he had never had problems reaching it.

He walked as quickly as he could while the sun was overhead but realized he was exhausting himself. There was no way he was getting home today. He would have to spend two nights out here no matter what he did, so he shouldn't push himself. He might need energy to fight the creature when it returned. It hadn't threatened him so far, but it might. Or there might be other, less friendly creatures.

As he walked – at a slower pace – he watched the sun begin its descent and wondered about the creature. Arlen, he supposed, though it seemed strange to give a creature a name. Humans had names, and humans gave names to other things, but other things didn't have their own names. It wasn't a common name but it also wasn't unusual. He would have expected an alien name from such a strange creature. The wind began to pick up as the sun fell and he shivered. It strummed against his ears and he waited for it to invade his mind and lead him to that creature. He blinked. The creature was in front of him on the path. Maybe the wind was driving him.

"I'm glad you stopped pushing yourself," the creature said,

coming to his side. He backed away and the creature looked annoyed. "Haven't you figured out that I'm not going to hurt you? Let me carry some of that for you. You can still walk for a few hours before you have to rest."

It was true, but there was no way he would give up the plants to this creature. He remained silent and the bags bumped against his legs as they had been all day. They went that way in silence for nearly twenty minutes before the bags tangled in his legs and he stumbled. It happened frequently but there wasn't usually anyone to see. The creature sighed.

"If you let me help, that wouldn't happen," he said. "I want you to get these plants back to your people. If I didn't, I wouldn't have let you harvest them. Please, let me help."

Jarl considered him. The creature could have stopped him easily and hadn't. But the creature had also snuck up on him and removed his mask. He kept walking.

"I have so many questions for you," the creature said. "Do you have any for me?"

Silence.

"You have the chance to talk to one of the creatures of this planet and you don't want to take advantage of it? I'm a little disappointed," the creature said. "Aren't you curious about this place? Aren't you curious about how humans can learn to live here?"

"How can you possibly feed on me without killing me?" he asked, because he did have a lot of questions and he had a feeling the creature was just going to keep bothering him until he started talking. The creature grinned as if pleased by his question.

"We adapt to the world around us," he said. "We feed on what is offered to us, but we have no way to connect with you humans except through flesh and your dreams. So those are the only things we can feed on. It's very limited. There has to be something else we can feed on that won't destroy you."

"But you don't know what it is?"

"When you're drawn to me, I'll feed on whatever you offer

me," the creature said, and he shivered. "Most humans offer their bodies because they can't imagine us wanting anything else. Some offer their nightmares because that's all they can imagine. If you imagine something different, something that you would survive, then you'll survive and we'll learn how to coexist with you."

"What else would you possibly want?"

"I don't know. I'm not human," the creature pointed out. "I don't know what you have to offer."

Jarl considered. There were stories of vampires from Earth, of creatures of the night who fed on blood, but he knew the creatures here already did that to some extent. They almost always found the bodies of those who were drawn out into the night, though they sometimes only found bones. Most of the bodies had been eaten, but some were drained of blood. The ones he didn't like to think about were the ones who seemed perfectly normal except liquid dripping from their ears. Autopsies had revealed that their brains had melted.

He stumbled again and the creature didn't say anything, just extended his hand. Jarl glared at him, but took a few of the bags from his back and handed them over without a word. The creature smiled and shouldered the bags the same way he held them and they began walking again.

"Didn't you say you had questions?" he finally asked, because he couldn't think of anything else to say and it was awkward walking with him without saying anything.

"Will you answer them?"

"I don't know. Maybe. Depends on what you ask."

"Where did you come from? Why are you here?"

"We came from a planet called Earth," he said, glancing over at the creature. "The humans there ruined the atmosphere, made it impossible to survive, but we fled before it was completely destroyed. We were looking for a new home where we could live without falling into those destructive patterns."

"You destroyed your previous home?" the creature asked in shock, coming to a stop. "Maybe we don't want you here."

"We know how to avoid it now," he said quickly, not wanting to make things worse for the humans here. "We learned. Humans learn from their mistakes. That will never happen here."

The creature narrowed his eyes. "So you say. Why should we trust you?"

"We're barely surviving here," he pointed out. "We're not powerful enough to damage this planet, and we can't control anything about it."

"How did you destroy your planet?"

"I'm not sure," he admitted. "The ancients hadn't discovered essence power yet, so they relied on energy that required huge amounts of gases to be produced. It unbalanced the planet. We discovered how to fix it but it was too late, and people had to leave. I don't know any more."

"You use this energy all the time, don't you?"

Jarl nodded. "But our energy is sustainable," he said. "It uses the sun. I don't know exactly how it works, but it isn't dangerous."

"You're sure?"

"We won't make the same mistake here," Jarl promised, and the creature began walking at his side again.

"Why did you choose this place as your home?"

"We didn't know how dangerous it was at first, so the first colonists took apart the ship that brought us here. Now we can't put it together to leave, so we're trapped. Why didn't you attack us at first? Were you trying to trap us here?"

"We thought you would leave," the creature said. "But you stayed, and we couldn't ignore you. Everything on this planet has to work together. There can't be parts of it that stand alone. That means we have to figure out how to integrate you into this world, but the only way we've found so far is quite unsatisfying. You're like a poison on our surface and we need to figure out what to do with you. It's quite troubling for us."

"You're not the ones getting killed," Jarl said bitterly.

The creature laughed, to his surprise. "We could do worse," he said. "We could lure all of you all at once. We're trying to be as gentle to you as we can while still fulfilling our biological imperative. And I'm trying to connect with you now so that you can survive and teach us a better way to feed."

"You actually want me to survive? Don't you like killing us?"

"No," he said. "If we wanted to kill you, we would. We want you to survive, but you have to become part of our planet. We need to neutralize your poison or find a way to adapt to it."

"If we're poison, why do you eat us?"

"Your bodies aren't poison," he said with a smile, flashing his fangs. "Your minds are."

Jarl shivered. The wind picked up and he flinched, looking around. But there was nothing for the wind to do, he realized. He was already walking next to the creature who would devour him. The wind didn't need to lure him anywhere. He eyed the creature and was again impressed at how handsome he was. And why was his skin so tan when he was a creature of the night? How was he possibly so human? If he were human, Jarl would be quite attracted to him, he realized. The creature glanced at him and smiled, revealing those fangs once again, and he shuddered. No, he was not attracted to this creature no matter how beautiful he was.

They walked in silence as the sunset faded into night, then he looked around. He needed to sleep if he wanted to be able to continue. He would need to walk all day tomorrow, then sleep out here again, but he would be back the next day. He was making good time and didn't need to push himself right now. He looked over at the creature, wondering if he would leave again or if he would sneak up on him in the middle of the night again.

"You need to sleep," the creature observed. "Have you seen any good places? There's somewhere nearby you might like."

"Where is it?" he asked warily, and the creature gestured off the path.

"It's in the woods about twenty minutes from here."

"I'm not leaving this trail."

"You'll be able to find your way back. I'll guide you." At Jarl's silence, he sighed. "If I wanted to lure you, you'd be dead. I just want you to have a good place where you can feel safe."

He wanted to point out that he wouldn't feel safe anywhere in these woods but didn't. This was the one time of year when he actually was safe, so he should try to relax. Maybe he did know a good place. He would try it.

He nodded and the creature led him off the path into the dense woods. He paused every so often to carve arrows into the trees and the creature looked amused but allowed it. He did not want to get lost here but he had to admit that if the creature was trying to kill him, there were easier ways of doing it. Then they reached a clearing and he exhaled in wonder.

The trees formed a perfect circle and the moon was perfectly framed overhead. It was a full moon, he realized as he stepped into the clearing and looked up. He had never seen the moon like this. It hung heavy in the sky and he realized he had never studied it before. Night was a time to be feared and the sight of the moon signaled danger, so he had never looked at it. The creature set his bags down and took Jarl's, who handed them over without protest, still entranced by the moon. Without a word, the creature lay down and crossed his arms behind his head, staring up at the beautiful orb. That was probably a better way to look at it, he considered, and lay down next to him, eyes still caught in the shining white globe.

"You've never really seen the moon, have you?"

"No," he whispered. "It's beautiful."

There were shadows across the surface and it almost looked like there were two rabbits chasing each other across the lower half, though they had to be craters. There were some who studied the moon, he knew, because the moon had such influence over the world here, but he had never paid attention. The moonlight held no warmth but it illuminated everything perfectly and he was amazed at how perfectly the trees framed it. The creature must have timed this perfectly to get him here right now and he was grateful he had followed.

"The moon is like a second mother to us," the creature said, still in that soft voice. It was like a seductive whisper.

"Our planet cares for us, but the moon guides us. She gives us strength, and wisdom. She counsels us. She is the one who pulls her power back so that you humans can safely travel for this short time each year. She wants to know you."

"It's just a moon," Jarl said cautiously, but looking at the beautiful moon, he did feel something mystical about it. He reached his hand up as if he could touch it and looked at the pale surface beyond his fingertips. His ancestors had traveled past that moon to get here, he thought. Had they found it as amazing as he did? Was that what had convinced them to stay? This gorgeous glowing sphere in the sky? He lowered his hand and noticed the creature looking at him with those ebony eyes. They were alien, but in that face they were nearly as lovely as the moon and he blushed and quickly looked away.

"Thank you for bringing me here," he said.

"Thank you for trusting me enough to leave your path, Jarl," the creature said. He shivered at how the creature caressed his name. "I'll leave you to sleep. There's no need to keep your mask on. It can't be comfortable. No one else will see you. I promise."

The creature got up and vanished into the ring of trees and he considered. There really was no point and it was uncomfortable. He got up and went to his bag to get ready to sleep and looked around. There really weren't any good nooks to hide in, but surely nothing would harm him. The moon had moved from the center of the circle of trees but he would like to look at it more. He went back to the center and lay on his back again, arms cushioning his head as he cautiously took off his mask and put it within arms reach.

He could see the moon completely now that the mask wasn't shielding the corners of his vision, and he let out a sigh of admiration. Was the moon capable of doing things? Was it an entity and not just a chunk of rock? Was it the reason he was safe right now, in the night on this treacherous planet? He stared at the moon for a long time and wasn't even aware of when he sank into sleep.

CHAPTER 4

Jarl opened his eyes and confusion swept over him. He looked around and put his mask back on, but he felt stunned. Two days left, he knew, but something had happened during the night. Or rather, nothing had happened. No nightmares. He knew he had slept, but he didn't remember anything other than a sweet melody that lingered in the back of his mind though he couldn't quite recall it. But he was still alive. He looked around. The moon was long gone but it was still dark and he wondered if the creature was nearby. He stood up and headed to the trees to relieve himself, then returned and looked around again. Was he supposed to leave? The creature had said he would guide him back. He waited a few minutes, then went to the bags and started hauling them up. He was glad he had thought to leave marks on the trees but where was the creature? He turned to leave and blinked. The creature was right in front of him.

"Miss me?" he said with that fang-baring smile.

"I thought you'd abandoned me without showing me the way back," Jarl said.

"I wouldn't leave you alone like that, Jarl," he said. "You have a long way to walk today."

He extended his hand towards the bags. "I can take more than you gave me yesterday. You might as well get my help while I'm still here."

Jarl barely even hesitated before he handed over most of the bags. If he was offering, he would accept the help. This was possibly the most important day of this entire venture. If he didn't get in a good twelve hours of walking today, then he would be cutting it close tomorrow. He had expected to arrive towards the evening tomorrow, but still with plenty of time before nightfall. That was how it usually worked out. If he had help, though, perhaps he could get back sooner. And if he took too long today, then he wouldn't be able to make up the time tomorrow and he wouldn't get back before the sun set and the woods returned to its usual malice. Although he supposed he already knew what would happen. He would be drawn to this creature. Still, he wanted to get the plants back to the colony before he was drawn back here.

The creature led him to the path and they began walking. He glanced over at the handsome form.

"Do you feed on our nightmares?" he asked, and the creature looked at him in surprise, then shrugged.

"It's possible. Sometimes that's all you offer us when you're drawn to us."

"Not those nightmares. The ones we have every night. Our usual sleep. Do you feed on that? Is that why you always give us nightmares?"

"The nightmares are your mind's attempt to make sense of the song of our planet," the creature said sadly. "She can't stop singing, but you can't seem to tolerate it. It's not meant to hurt you."

"A song?" he asked in surprise, thinking of the melody that was the only thing he remembered from his dreams. Had he heard the planet's song? That would explain why he didn't have nightmares, he supposed. If the nightmares were a result of his inability to process the song, then maybe he had just processed it correctly last night. He wondered if other people sometimes heard a song. He knew sometimes people claimed to have no memory of their nightmares, so maybe the same thing that had happened to him last night happened to them.

"I would sing it to you, but I think you'd go insane," the creature said with a grin. "I don't want to risk that."

"Thanks," Jarl muttered, though he wondered. If he had heard the song last night, would it drive him insane? Probably, he admitted. It had been a fluke that he heard it and it would never happen again. He supposed he would find out tonight. If he heard the song again, then something had changed, but if he had nightmares again, then it was just a one-time occurrence.

The horizon was getting lighter and he glanced at the creature.

"Don't you have to leave?"

"Ready for me to go?" the creature teased. "I thought you appreciated the help."

"I do," he assured him. "But you can't be in the sun, can you?"

"I prefer not to be, but there's nothing stopping me," he said. "I'm just weaker than usual. It's the only time you humans are able to kill us."

"I'm not going to kill you."

"If you killed me, you wouldn't be drawn back here once the moon returns her power. I'm the only one drawing you."

Jarl stumbled to a halt and stared at him. Was that true? The creature looked at him expressionlessly as his hand went to the gun at his side. If he killed this creature, he might live. There was still a chance another creature would entrap him, but he might survive this. But could he kill this creature? He had never killed like this before. He had killed animals, but never people. And even though this was a creature, it was also a person. He couldn't kill someone who had been helping him the past two days. His hand lowered. Killing him might save his life, but he couldn't do it.

The creature had come to a stop when he did, and set the bags down.

"Thank you, Jarl," the creature said seriously. "I'll be back when it's dark."

"I'll see you then," Jarl said, and the creature smiled at him.

"Call me Arlen."

Jarl stared into those enticing ebony eyes. It was hard to read emotions in those eyes and he supposed that was why the creature smiled so often. There were few other ways to indicate that he didn't mean any harm or that he was amused. The fangs weren't reassuring, but there weren't any other good ways to express emotions when it was so difficult to read his eyes. He smiled hesitantly.

"All right, Arlen," he said, and the creature grinned before heading off into the woods.

He picked up the bags that the creature – Arlen – had been carrying and readjusted them, then set off. He needed to make good time and if there was ever a time to push himself, it was today. He couldn't go too hard, but he needed to be mostly home by the time the sun went down. As he walked, he wondered about the song in his dreams and the lack of nightmares, and about Arlen. He seemed sincere enough. Had Jarl made a mistake in leaving him alive? He wasn't sure. Arlen didn't want to kill him, after all. He wanted him to survive. Maybe he would survive. No one ever had, but that didn't mean it was impossible. It would depend on what he offered when Arlen drew him in.

He wondered how it would happen. Would Arlen ask him what he wanted to give? Somehow he didn't think that was how it worked. Surely if the creatures operated like that, other people would have survived. It was probably instinctive, or unconscious, or something he had no control over. He knew that once people heard the lure, they lost all rational thought. If the guards could keep them from going into the woods then they recovered in the daylight. Most didn't try to go back the next night but some did. If a creature had seen a person's face, then they were drawn every night until they finally escaped. He suspected that would happen to him. Arlen had seen his face after all, and heard his voice, and knew his name. Would he be aware of it when he lost control and was driven to go into the woods at night? Or would everything go blank? Maybe it just felt like falling asleep except you never woke up.

The day passed in a blur of exhaustion. His lunch break was short and he hated eating the rations when he was carrying such delicious pollen, but the pollen was for the future. He was allowed to taste it to make sure it was ripe, but other than that, it had to arrive in perfect condition. The rest of the colony relied on him, so he choked down the dry rations with a swig of water and rested for a little bit before starting again. By the time the sun was sinking into the horizon, his legs were aching.

He and the others trained for these expeditions all year, since it was five days of nonstop walking, but no amount of training fully prepared him. There were only so many places to go in the colony and no real opportunities to train in real world conditions. Every year he was amazed at how underprepared he was, but he always made it back with time to spare. He had made good time today, he thought as the sun sank lower. Even if he went to sleep now he would be on track, and he could easily keep walking another hour or two.

The wind picked up but for once, it didn't terrify him. All it could do was bring him to Arlen and he was already looking for him to show up. He heard the familiar clopping and paused, looking around. He didn't see anything. He kept going, wondering if there was a reason he hadn't shown up. The hairs on the back of his neck stood up as the clopping stopped abruptly. This didn't feel right. He heard another noise at his side and whirled. He gasped.

There was a creature partially hidden in the trees to his right. It wasn't Arlen. His hand went to his gun automatically as he let the bags drop, crouching and aiming at her even though he knew it wouldn't help. She stared at him, then bared her fangs. It wasn't a smile.

He shivered. She was as beautiful as Arlen but she was cold and her ebony eyes had no humor in them. He realized with a start that he had been able to read emotion in Arlen, because he could clearly read this woman's hostility. She was tall, like Arlen, and had the same eyes and long fingers. Her skin was equally bronzed and her features were equally striking. She wore the same type of draping cloth outfit but hers exposed a luscious female figure and he clenched his gun tighter as terror swept through him. His mask was on, he thought desperately. She couldn't see him. Couldn't draw him in. And the planet was still safe for another night and day.

He backed up nervously and ran into something. His heart skipped a beat and he whirled, bringing the gun up- and stopped. It was Arlen. He had never felt so relieved to see someone. Arlen was looking at the woman, not at him, and there was ice in his eyes equal to hers. Jarl shivered, but it wasn't directed at him.

"Leave," Arlen said to the woman. "You have no business with him. He's intended for me."

She hissed and Jarl backed into Arlen further, seeking protection from him. Arlen wrapped an arm around his waist, his eyes still fixed on the woman.

"Leave," he repeated.

She eyed him and bared her fangs again, then turned and vanished into the woods. Arlen waited for a long moment as Jarl remained in his embrace, terrified. Then Arlen released him and picked up his bags, handing him two and keeping the rest for himself. Jarl took them with trembling hands.

"Thank you, Arlen," he whispered.

The creature studied him, then his lips curled into a smile.

"You called me Arlen."

"You said I should."

"I didn't expect you to, even if I asked."

"Who was that? Why was she here?"

Arlen was silent for a moment, then gestured for them to start walking. He obeyed, grateful that Arlen was at his side.

"Many of us are curious about you," he explained. "You're the first human who's talked to us."

"I thought you hadn't tried before."

"We've tried a couple of times, but not the way I did," Arlen said. "We usually just threaten. No one else has bothered with a friendly approach."

"Thank you for not threatening me," he said with a shiver. He had been so terrified the first time he saw Arlen, even though he knew the creature couldn't hurt him right now. Seeing the woman had brought back the terror. "So you do hate humans and want to eat us."

"I don't," he said firmly.

"But she does," he pointed out, because there was no denying the hostility in her gaze. "When you summon me back out here, after this safety is over, will she be there?"

"She may be," he admitted. Jarl shivered. "But you will be drawn to me and only me. You are intended for me."

"So I'll be safe?"

Arlen looked at him in surprise. "Safe?"

Of course he wouldn't be safe, Jarl realized with a blush. He would be walking into his death. It was easy to forget because Arlen was protecting him right now, and he felt close to him thanks to their conversation, but Arlen was going to devour him. He would either feast on his flesh or his mind and Jarl would be dead. Still…

"You said I might survive," he said cautiously. "And everyone is drawn to the woods eventually. I'd rather have it be you than anyone else."

Jarl lips curled again. Maybe he had realized that smiling the way he normally did exposed his fangs and frightened Jarl, he realized. Maybe that was why he wasn't fully smiling. But while the sight of those fangs was off-putting, he found he missed Arlen's constant good humor. It was irritating at time, but made him feel safer. Arlen wasn't a threat when he was smiling, fangs or no.

"I hope this experiment works," Arlen said. "You humans are fascinating. I would like to keep talking to you beyond tomorrow."

"Couldn't you just not kill me?"

"It's not my choice," Arlen said. "You'll be drawn to the woods and you'll offer something to me, and I'll be compelled to take it. Neither of us have any choice in the matter."

"So I won't be able to choose what to offer?" he asked, thinking of his questions earlier.

"No," Arlen said. "I don't know how humans determine what to offer, but it isn't their choice. It just happens."

"And you can't choose to refuse? Even if you don't want to kill me?"

"If you offer me something that doesn't kill you, I won't," Arlen said. "Do you know something you could offer?"

"Not really," Jarl admitted. The bags banged into his legs and he adjusted them. It was much easier with only two bags but still clumsy. Arlen was carrying far more bags than he had before and they were making good time now. He would try to walk as long as possible, he decided. He wouldn't need much rest tonight because tomorrow, he would be home. This would be his last night, he realized. Tomorrow night he would be drawn back out here into the unknown. The guards might stop him for a night or two but he would come back here and see Arlen again. He found he wasn't nearly as frightened of that thought as he had been. Even if he died, at least he would see a friendly face first. That was far better than his other options.

They walked in silence for a time, then heard clopping behind them. Jarl tensed and dropped into a crouch, reaching for his gun. Arlen turned and stared into the woods, and the sound stopped.

"They won't come near when I'm with you," Arlen said. He was glaring into the darkness. Arlen wondered if he could see the other creature. He hadn't put his night goggles on yet because the moon was so bright he could still see fairly well and he knew they wouldn't work on creatures. It ought to be darker, he realized. Why wasn't it? It was almost as if the moonlight was being magnified around him so he could see the surrounding area, but the woods were nearly pitch black. That was how everything should be. He glanced at Arlen. Was it because of him? Did his presence make the moonlight stronger? The creatures were closely associated with the moon, after all. He had even said they drew power from the moon. Maybe it made sense that things were easier to see around him.

He straightened and they kept walking. Soon he was looking for a place to sleep and fear was creeping up on him. Arlen was looking around, too, and then pointed to a clearing at the side of the path with a hollow that would be perfect for sleeping. Jarl nodded and they both set the bags down beside the spot. Jarl eyed the woods around him, then Arlen.

"Will you stay with me, Arlen?" he asked, and the creature looked surprised.

"You want me to stay?"

"You said no one would come near if you're here," he explained. "I won't feel safe if you leave."

"I've been fairly close to you every night," Arlen said. "Surely you realize that. Even during the day I trail you."

"I want you here, within sight," Jarl said.

Arlen grinned, his usual grin that exposed his fangs, and the sight reassured rather than terrified him. He smiled cautiously in return.

"Of course," he said.

Jarl went to his personal bag and got ready to sleep quickly, then headed a short distance away to relieve himself and paused. He didn't like going so far and gestured for Arlen to join him. The creature obeyed, and looked at him curiously as he exposed himself and went.

"I had wondered what that was for," he said, and Jarl looked at him in surprise as he zipped his pants again. He slept in his clothes these five days since no one wanted to risk changing in the dangerous woods. This was the only time he exposed his body and he realized Arlen had never seen him.

"Don't you use the bathroom?"

"No," Arlen said. "Our waste is exuded into the air."

"What?" Jarl said, drawing back slightly. Was he breathing in human waste? Creature waste, he corrected. Still undesirable.

Arlen laughed. "Not around others," he said. "And not with the frequency you humans seem to have."

Jarl's brow creased. "If you don't use it for that, what do you use it for? Sex?"

"We don't have sex," the creature said, and Jarl puzzled.

"Then how do you create more of yourselves?"

"We spawn from human dreams," he explained. "I spawned

from your dreams. That's why you're intended for me."

Jarl blinked and drew back, his fear of the creature suddenly returning. This creature was drawn from his nightmares? But he looked nothing like any of the nightmares he had ever had. He was far too handsome.

"You don't look like anything I fear," he said cautiously.

"All of your dreams, not just your nightmares," Arlen said with that smile. Despite the fangs, it was hard to stay terrified when the creature looked so friendly. All of his dreams? That implied his desires as well as his fears and he examined Arlen again. He had to admit that Arlen was exactly his type. He had always been drawn to men, and Arlen was perfect. If it weren't for those few alien traits that marked him as a creature, he would be Jarl's ideal. He blushed and wondered what the others would think, seeing exactly what Jarl dreamed about. It was almost a violation of his privacy to have his desires brought to life like this.

"Do you not like this body?" Arlen asked, as if picking up on his hesitance. "I can probably change it, but the only way I know how to do that is to draw on your nightmares and I doubt you want that."

"I don't want you to change," Jarl admitted. "You're perfect the way you are. I just don't want anyone else to see you. Dreams are meant to be private."

"Yet you impose them on the world around you constantly," Arlen said. "You're a poison, and we're just trying to adapt."

"Did you exist before we came here?" he asked curiously. If Arlen were drawn from his dreams and was an attempt by the planet to deal with human dreams, then that implied the species hadn't been around long. The plants apparently also hadn't been there before humans, he remembered. "How do things evolve so quickly here?"

"Our planet produces what it needs," Arlen said with a shrug.

"But you're an individual, right? Not some sort of collective consciousness?"

"I am me," Arlen said with another laugh. "It's true that before my type of people, we were a collective consciousness. But we're unique, because your dreams are unique. We're still connected to the world, but we're independent. I like it," he added. "I like being myself."

"I'm glad," Jarl said, wondering what it would be like not to have freedom of thought, to belong to some greater mind. Did it feel like a singular mind? Did each creature perceive itself to be in control? Or did they each have a mind that was controlled by the collective mind? He shivered. He hoped he never found out.

Then he went to the hollow and lay down. He looked for the moon but didn't see it. It was hidden behind the trees and he was sad. He would have liked to spend more time looking at it, because it was likely the last chance he would get. Arlen sat down next to him and reached out to caress his head. It felt good and Jarl didn't resist.

"I'll watch over you, Jarl," he said softly. "I won't leave your side."

"Thank you, Arlen," he whispered, then shut his eyes and fell into sleep. Teeth flashed into his dreams but while he was usually terrified of them, he was almost comforted. Threads of fear wound through him as the woods loomed large in his nightmares but again, it was almost comforting. Arlen waited in the woods. It was no longer an unknown death that haunted his dreams but a certain one, certain not just because he couldn't escape it but because he no longer wanted to. He woke refreshed and he felt strange. Like yesterday morning, there was no lingering fear from his nightmares. He felt only content and saw Arlen waiting in the exact same spot. This was the last day of the peace.

CHAPTER 5

Arlen carried most of the bags again without hesitation and Jarl realized he was making very good time. Normally he would arrive towards evening but it would be afternoon at the pace they were making. The colony would be surprised and pleased to get the pollen pods so early. Their supplies always started running low before the planet subdued enough to let them leave to harvest the plants and they would be pleased.

"What will you tell them?" Arlen asked. They had been chatting casually since he had woken up, but this question was a good one. What would he tell them?

"I'm not sure," he admitted. Was it safe to reveal that he had spent so much time with a creature? Should he tell them what he had learned? Or would that endanger Arlen in some way? He glanced at Arlen. The tall alien was shouldering all but two of the bags with no difficulty and because he was so tall, the bags didn't tangle in his legs the way they did with Jarl. He noticed Jarl's attention and smiled.

"Why wouldn't you tell them everything?"

"I don't want you in danger," he said.

"As long as I don't show myself in the daylight, I'm not in danger," he pointed out.

"I suppose that's true," he said, considering. "But they might kill me if they find out. You're supposed to be an enemy."

"I would think they would be happy that a creature is offering them peace," Arlen said.

"You don't know humans," Jarl said, thinking of the terror others would feel hearing that a creature had approached them. They wouldn't understand how a creature could be friendly. All they knew was a century of fear and hate. It would take time for them to recognize that not all creatures were unspeakably evil, and he didn't have that time. Tomorrow night he would be drawn out. He shivered, but it was no longer the same fear. At least he would see Arlen again.

"You have to go soon, don't you?" he asked, because the sun was nearly at the horizon. Arlen glanced at it.

"I can stay a little longer, if you like."

"Aren't you in danger?"

"Not from you," Arlen said with a smile. "Or have you changed your mind?"

"No," he said softly. "I don't want to kill you."

They walked further as the sun began to rise, talking to each other. It was odd how easy it was to talk to him. He was curious about everything and Jarl told him some of the history of the colony, though it felt odd to be telling him. Most of their history involved strategies for getting rid of the plants and animals and defending themselves from the horror of this place, but Arlen was part of this world and was probably offended. He looked curious, though, not angry, so Jarl told him everything he could think of. He wasn't well-versed in their history but knew the basics, and knew their current society. Still, Arlen knew nothing, so he was almost an expert when compared to someone with no knowledge whatsoever.

When the sun had fully come over the horizon, Arlen sighed.

"I need to leave now," he said. "We're close enough that there might be others returning, or out on patrol. I can't risk it, though I would love to hear more."

"Then I suppose I'll see you tonight," Jarl said, and Arlen grinned.

"I suppose you will, or some night very soon. You're not afraid?"

"Not anymore."

"Good," Arlen said. "Maybe you'll survive."

He set the bags down and Jarl set his bags down as well, then extended his hand. Arlen looked at it in confusion for a moment, then cautiously took it. Jarl shook it firmly, tempted to pull the creature into a hug. But he would leave it as a handshake. Arlen probably wouldn't understand the difference between a handshake and a hug in terms of the intimacy it implied but Jarl did, and he didn't want to cross any lines. Arlen was right. There might be other humans around, and he didn't want them to see him hugging a creature even if that was his instinct.

"Goodbye for now, Jarl," Arlen said with another fang-baring smile.

"Goodbye for now, Arlen," he responded, again tempted to hug him. Arlen had kept him safe and helped him return with hours to spare. He would only have to walk a few hours on his own and he would be home. The creature turned and faded into the darkness of the woods and Jarl picked up all the bags, again reminded of how awkward they all were. Arlen really had been doing him a favor by carrying these, he thought as they tangled in his legs almost immediately. He reorganized everything and headed off towards the colony.

When he drew close enough to see the metal glinting through the thinning trees, he came across the first humans sawing down the trees. Each year they went out to try to get rid of as many trees as possible. They wanted the woods as far from them as possible and this was the only time of year it was safe to spend extended time out here. The trees regrew quickly and it was a hopeless task, but the trees were noticeably thinner as he approached.

"Is that you, Jarl?" someone called, and he saw one of his friends weighed down with bags just like him on another path near him. Kandor, who had gone to another patch and was one of Jarl's dearest friends. His patch was the second farthest out and he wondered if he had also met with a creature. Maybe Arlen wasn't the only one trying to make contact, though that hadn't occurred to him before. He felt a surprising flash of jealousy at the thought of other creatures making contact. He wanted to be special, for his relationship with Arlen to be special.

"You made good time," Kandor continued, setting his bags down and extending his arms for a hug. Jarl set his bags down as well and embraced him tightly. Kandor looked human, and it was rather jarring after seeing only Arlen these past few days.

"I got tangled up less than usual," he said with perfect honesty, though he didn't want to get into the specifics of why that was.

"Let's go show the others what we found," Kandor said with a smile. "Did you get the full harvest?"

"Every plant was ripe," he confirmed. "How about you?"

"One wasn't," he said with a sigh. "It happens so rarely, but nothing to be done except wait for next year. It shouldn't matter. Even in the years when there isn't a full harvest we always manage to hang on. And there's always the reserves. I just hope everyone else is as successful as you."

They approached the heavily fortified gates of the colony, which were open because the sun was high in the sky and it was still the safe period. Starting tonight, they would be firmly shut except for the few daytime excursions the colonists made. Others began crowding around them as they approached the sorting facility, people congratulating them and admiring their full bags. Jarl especially got compliments for arriving so quickly and he wondered what they would say if they knew how he had gotten here. Would they accept that he had befriended one of the creatures or would they shun him? Would they exile him? He shivered. If they exiled him, what would happen if one of the other creatures found him before Arlen did? He doubted any other creature would be as friendly.

"Kandor, welcome home," a voice said. "Jarl, you made good time."

The head of processing grinned at them and for a moment, Jarl felt a flash of sorrow that it was such a human expression. But he smiled in return and they went into the facility to unload their pollen pods. Everyone inside helped them sort the pods out. The ones they had tested would be eaten first, as the skin had already been punctured and they would only last a couple of weeks. The others went into storage.

Everyone commiserated with Kandor on the unripened fruit in his patch and informed them that everyone else had returned. Two others had incomplete harvests, but they felt confident they would survive. There were always a certain number of pods they held in case of emergency. They were rotated out every year so they would be fresh and he knew that even if a harvest failed entirely, they would be able to survive on reduced rations until the next year. The processors were extremely wise with how they doled out the pods and they relied on other food as much as possible.

As they processed the pods, one of the old timers came over. His name was Doss and he had been a harvester. He was the one to prepare them each year, helping them train and keep in shape so they would be able to get to the patches and back in time. He clapped Jarl on the shoulder and congratulated his speed, and Jarl wondered what he would think about the creatures. He considered. This was one of the old timers who had once seen a creature, he knew. The man had spoken of it in whispers. Surely he could be trusted a little.

"How did you make such good time?" the man asked. "I must have done an especially good job training you last year."

"I saw a creature," he started hesitantly, and the man's eyes widened as he inhaled sharply.

"A creature? But you're safe?"

"Yes," Jarl said, wondering if should expand on that. Doss chuckled.

"I was quick the year I saw one, too. They're fearsome, aren't they? Like nightmares brought to life. I'm glad you didn't lose or harm any of the pods in your haste. I dropped two of mine that year."

"It wasn't as terrifying as I thought it would be," he said, wondering if he should go farther.

"You're a braver man than me," the old timer laughed. "But

don't tell the others. I don't want them hesitating next year. In time, when you're old like me, you can tell them. But not yet."

He nodded. Best not to explain then. If he wasn't even supposed to mention it to the others, then he wouldn't explain that he had actually talked to the creature and he wasn't frightening at all. He wondered, though. Arlen had said he was drawn from all of Jarl's dreams but the old timer said it was like a nightmare. Did the creatures used to base themselves off nightmares alone? And was the creature the old timer saw the one that was spawned from his dreams or a different one?

He hadn't been drawn into the woods yet so Jarl had to assume it wasn't the one he was intended for. He shivered at the thought that everyone here had a creature spawned from them who was waiting to lure them out into the woods. Some people escaped, he knew. Some people died natural deaths, and not just accidental deaths. Some people died of old age. They were honored. It was a feat few accomplished, but it wasn't impossible.

As he headed to his home on the outskirts of the colony, he wondered what would happen tonight. He knew he would be drawn out, but would the guards stop him or would he slip through? His mind was a whirl all day and when he got ready for bed, he was careful to get in his best pajamas. After all, Arlen might see them and he wanted to look good. He got into bed and shut his eyes as the wind began to pick up outside. He shivered and felt the stirrings in his mind. The peace was over and the wind was no longer harmless. He wondered how many others would be driven to seek the woods tonight. It always seemed to be more than usual right after a peace.

The wind increased and he heard it clearly in his mind. It was the same song he had heard while sleeping under the moon, he realized. He hadn't been able to remember it after that night but hearing it now, he recognized it instantly. It was a siren's call, driving him to action. He was vaguely aware of getting up, of going to the door. So he would be aware of this. He wasn't sure how to feel about that but it did mean he would be at least somewhat conscious when he saw Arlen again. That gave him some relief. But it was eery watching his body move without his command. Perhaps this was how the other creatures of the planet felt as their actions were dictated by the collective consciousness of the planet. It was a strange feeling of helplessness and inevitability. He was under the planet's spell and the song wound through his with increasing urgency.

Someone grabbed him just as he reached the walls. A guard.

"I have to leave," he murmured, trying to push past the guard.

"No, you don't," the guard said gently, though Jarl knew there was no point trying to persuade those driven to leave. No one had ever been talked out of it. They could only stop them physically. Besides, he didn't want to be talked out of this. He wanted to go to the woods. He wanted to see Arlen.

"He's waiting for me," he tried, but the guard sighed and gripped him tighter. How did others get past? He heard the song pick up again and suddenly the guard winced and released him, falling to the ground. Had he hurt the guard? He knew they were attacked but he wasn't even aware of attacking him. He kept walking. It was possible to survive the drop from the wall, he knew. No one knew how people survived it but everyone did when they were called to the woods. Everyone survived long enough to get there, and then they died. Always.

Another body tackled him and this time he was aware of fighting, but there were two bodies on him, then three. He fought but it did nothing. Handcuffs were put on him and he broke them apart with a strength he shouldn't have possessed. Nothing would stop him from following the siren's song and getting to Arlen. He was aware of constant people pulling him back and grew desperate. He needed to get through. And then something broke through the song. It fractured and he flinched. The song driving his actions was gone and he was suddenly in control of his body. He looked around.

Four guards surrounded him, two of them holding their sides as if injured. They watched him warily and he looked to see that the sun had broken the horizon. He slumped down. They had successfully stopped him and he didn't know how to feel.

“He’s back,” one of the guards said. “Get him back to his home. He’ll sleep it off safely.”

CHAPTER 6

Jarl opened his eyes to the sun streaming in. No nightmares. Or at least they weren't nightmares anymore. Just like the night before, he had dreamed of the usual shapes and figures but they hadn't filled him with fear. Last night, they had filled him with longing. That was this morning, he supposed as he stretched and got ready for the day. The night had been his attempt to get to Arlen. He couldn't quite remember the melody that had lured him and he wondered why not. As soon as the sun had fractured the notes, they had vanished from his memory.

He had no responsibilities for the first week after he returned, he knew. Going out to harvest the plants was a dangerous task and those who completed it were rewarded with this short break from their duties. Normally everyone pitched in with the basic functioning of the colony. He was almost always helping with the cooking, as he had a knack for it, but he was sometimes sent to clean out the animal pens. That was one of the least desirable jobs and everyone rotated so no single person would get stuck with it. There were a few jobs like that but it would probably be a month before he had to spend a week in muck. He was also responsible for keeping himself in shape and then, in six months, his formal training would begin again to prepare him for next year.

Only there wouldn't be a next year. At some point the guards would slip up and he would be drawn into the woods. Should he warn the old timer who was in charge of preparing them?

They had young people in training to take over in case anything happened to them while harvesting the plants, but none would be ready to take on the furthest path without serious training. Well, he likely wouldn't last long and they would get their full year of training and be prepared.

As he left his home, he was surprised to see the old timer waiting outside. The man nodded to him, then gestured for him to follow. He was taken to the president's house at the center of town. He had been here before; his job as a harvester gave him quite a few honors and all harvesters were sometimes recognized for their hard work. But it was usually on the day they returned, not the day after. The president was waiting for them and she smiled broadly as they approached, waving for them to sit in the comfortable chairs scattered around one side of the room where the old timers often sat and helped the president lead the colony. Jarl sat uncomfortably, not sure what this was about.

"You were lured out last night," the president said. "Do you remember?"

"Vaguely," he said, because he couldn't remember it clearly.

"Doss here says you saw a creature. The year after he saw a creature, he was drawn for days before he was able to control himself."

Jarl looked at the man in surprise, wondering why he hadn't said anything or warned him in any way. The old timer sighed.

"You're wondering why I didn't tell you, aren't you," he said. "Well, I was hoping it wouldn't happen to you. You'll be under watch the next week or so. I don't think we could have stopped you last night if I hadn't warned the president. It took four of them to keep me back, too."

"Is that unusual?"

"Normally a single guard can stop people," the president said. "But we'll keep four focused on you until this passes. It'll weaken our guard elsewhere, but we'll risk it."

"You can't do that," he said, shocked. "You can't risk other lives just to save mine. I'm just one person."

"You're one important person," the president pointed out. "Perhaps the most important. The long path is difficult to manage and you're the only one trained for it."

"We're all equal," he pointed out, repeating one of their basic lessons. Every citizen of the colony was equal. Some had more influence in certain areas due to their ability or experience, but everyone had equal rations and equal protection against the night, and everyone shared equal responsibilities to some extent. Even the president worked with the animals sometimes, he knew. Everyone was equal.

The president laughed, as did the old timer.

"I wish that were true," she said. "And we do our best to meet that standard. But we're not equal, and you're too important to lose. We'll keep guarding you as long as it takes no matter who it puts at risk."

Jarl was silent. That was not good. He would never stop being drawn. He didn't want to stop. He wanted to go to the woods and see Arlen. And he did not want other people at risk because of him. He might survive; the others wouldn't. He thought of the female creature he had seen and shivered. They would be going to that fate. His fate with Arlen was far better, but he didn't know how to explain it to them.

"That creature I saw," he said hesitantly. "I don't think he was threatening me."

Would he be able to explain this to them? Would he be able to persuade them to let him leave?

The old timer snorted.

"Of course it wasn't," he said. "It was a peace. It's the one time they don't threaten us. But if you saw it, then it saw you and it's going to try to draw you until it gives up. Don't worry," he added. "Mine gave up after a week, but most give up after a single night. This is only temporary."

Jarl nodded, unsure what else to do. The president congratulated him again on a successful harvest and the old timer led him out.

"Take some time to relax," he said. "You've earned it. And tonight, you'll be under guard again. Don't worry. We won't let you be eaten."

He smiled weakly as the old timer walked away. Was there any way to explain this to them? To tell them what Arlen was really like? He couldn't risk it. They might put him under even heavier guard and he couldn't allow that. Could he get by four guards? He wasn't sure but he would certainly try.

He spent the day visiting with his neighbors, enjoying the freedom from work and knowing this was probably the last chance he would get to visit with everyone like this. He got ready for bed carefully again, cleaning himself thoroughly and getting into his best pajamas again. He closed his eyes and visions of gnashing fangs filled his mind, tinged with sadness. Wisps fluttered past him and he reached for them, but couldn't get to them. And then he opened his eyes. It was morning.

He looked around, wondering if he had tried to leave and just didn't remember it. He got ready for the day and came out to see the old timer again, who grinned at him.

"Looks like the creature gave up," he said. "You got lucky. We'll leave the guards tonight as well, but you should be fine."

"Thanks," Jarl said, unsure what else to say. Had Arlen really given up? That easily? No, he had said that the guards might stop him for a week but he would still be drawn. What was going on? Did Arlen no longer want him? His heart clenched. He ought to be happy that he was being spared this fate but he had come to terms with it, wanted it even. How could a creature spawned from his dreams no longer want him?

He went through the day in a daze and the next night passed uneventfully, only his dreams were almost nightmares because of the pained longing in them. Had he somehow failed? Was Arlen angry that he hadn't been able to break free from the guards that first night? They had spent several days together and it had felt like they connected; was that broken now?

That night he got into regular pajamas. The guards had been reassigned and he wouldn't be drawn to the woods again. Arlen wasn't interested anymore, though he wasn't sure why. He felt like he had failed in some way and couldn't explain the sense of loss he felt with anyone else. Everyone had known that he had been drawn and Kandor had even asked him about it in a low voice, but he had said he didn't remember clearly. He didn't. Maybe he had done something wrong when he had been drawn. Maybe he hadn't reacted the way he was supposed to react. As his eyes shut, he knew he was in for another round of unsatisfied dreams.

CHAPTER 7

Music filled his mind and he sat up in a trance. The song of the planet wailed like a siren in his mind and he recognized it instantly. How was it that he kept forgetting what it sounded like? It was so irresistible, so unique. He would never forget it again, he knew. He felt his body get up and head towards the wall. No guards were in sight as he reached the wall and, without any hesitation, stepped off. He was trapped inside his mind and watched with fear as the ground approached and he knew he would be dashed to pieces, but then the air seemed to thicken and slow him, and he stumbled to the ground. His body stood back up. He wasn't in control and it was terrifying. How had he forgotten how frightening it was to be caught up in the music like this?

The woods seemed to part before him and his body seemed to know exactly where to go as he climbed over fallen trees in the areas that weren't on the paths, the areas people didn't dare go. It was pitch black and terror filled him. He couldn't see anything but his body climbed regardless, in the thrall of some darkness he had never imagined. Then it began to lighten. The moonlight intensified and suddenly he saw a creature before him. The female. She needed his flesh and he offered himself to her without a thought, stepping forward so she could feast on him.

"Stop," a voice said sharply and he turned. Arlen. He barely had time for relief because Arlen needed him, too. He needed to offer his body to Arlen, but not in the same way. He needed to offer his heart as well, he realized, and went up to the creature without hesitation. He wrapped his arms around Arlen's tall shoulders and stood on his tiptoes to kiss the creature, not caring about his fangs or alien nature or anything else. He needed Arlen to take him. He needed to offer himself to the creature's hunger and this was what the creature needed.

Arlen leaned down to make the kiss easier for him and his mouth opened, his tongue snaking into Jarl's mouth. But Jarl's tongue caught on his fangs and his mouth filled with blood, and he pulled away. Arlen didn't need blood. He needed his heart, and his body. Not blood. He took Arlen's hand and placed it on his heart, doing everything in his power to give Arlen the love and lust flowing through him so that it could feed Arlen and give him what he needed. He offered everything and felt Arlen feeding through the hand on his chest, but it wasn't enough. He needed to give Arlen his body as well.

Without thought, he began tearing at his pajamas and then at Arlen's draping clothing until they were both naked. The mere touch of Arlen's cool skin against his set his body on fire and he moaned as Arlen wrapped one arm around his waist, his other hand still over his heart. Arlen lowered them to the ground until he was over Jarl and Jarl wrapped his leg around Arlen's, desperate to give himself to the creature. He needed to give his body to him and now he could feel Arlen's arousal against him.

This wasn't his first time with a man by any means, but he had never felt anything like this. He was desperate for Arlen, needed him, and this was taking too long. He grabbed the creature and pulled him towards him, but Arlen didn't seem to know what to do or else he was deliberately delaying. He vaguely remembered that the creatures didn't have sex, that Arlen hadn't known what a penis was for. That was a problem because he needed to offer his body to Arlen and he needed to do it quickly.

He pulled his legs up and reached to feel Arlen's powerful cock, then, carefully, pulled him into position. This was going to hurt, he suspected, but he didn't care. He wanted this so badly. Every fiber of his being ached with the need. He could feel Arlen feeding on his heart but he needed to feed on his body, too. Luckily, Arlen finally seemed to understand what he was supposed to do and the creature lowered one hand to trace down to Jarl's opening. He pressed his cock against Jarl and he whimpered with need, but Arlen hesitated. Precum coated his opening and Arlen's fingers soothed it, but he wanted Arlen inside him. Now.

He arched his back and then Arlen pressed down on his hips, stroking his cock and finally, finally, entering him. He gasped in relief and pleasure as Arlen slid into him, the sensation far better than anything he had ever experienced because he could finally feel Arlen feeding on his body as he needed to do. He offered his body to Arlen and Arlen took it, shoving into him with a jolt and then beginning a pulsing pattern that filled Jarl with an aching pleasure. He bore down on the massive cock, needing to feel every inch as it pulsed in and out of his body, and could feel a drag against his senses that he knew was Arlen feeding.

One of Arlen's hands was still on his heart and now he was feeding on everything Jarl was offering him, heart and body. He felt complete in a way he never had, satisfied even though his body was still purring with pleasure. The completion sparked deep within him and he cried out as his cock spasmed into an orgasm so pure he could hardly comprehend it. But Arlen kept going, and he needed Arlen to keep going. It lasted and lasted, and then Arlen gasped against him and something exploded deep inside him. Arlen kept his hand on Jarl's chest as he pulled out, but Jarl was still desperate.

"Again," he whispered, and without a word, Arlen entered him.

He didn't even wonder how Arlen was ready to go so quickly; he needed this and Arlen was giving it to him. He reached his peak twice more before Arlen reached his. Again. He pleaded and begged and Arlen took him again. And again. His body ached and felt battered, and he knew he couldn't stand anymore. But he still ached with the need to offer himself. He would keep giving himself to Arlen until his body failed, he knew. He would still need it until his final resources failed. And then he looked beyond Arlen and saw the moon. He drew in a slow breath, entranced and distracted from the lust that filled him.

The song in his mind that had continued to drive him quieted for a moment as the glow of the moon soothed his senses and calmed his body. Arlen was looking at him in concern, he realized, still with one hand on his heart, still feeding but no longer inside him.

"Jarl," he said. "Can you hear me?"

Jarl couldn't speak, too caught up in the moon. It was so beautiful. Arlen had shown him the moon for the first time and he couldn't believe he had never studied it before. The music in his mind slowed to a quiet twinkling of notes in the back of his mind and he took a sudden breath. He looked around, suddenly realizing what was happening and back in control of his mind.

"Jarl," Arlen repeated, sounding panicked.

"I hear you," he said, breaking his gaze from the moon to look straight at Arlen, who looked almost shocked. His body ached and he knew it would be days before he was able to sit comfortably. Why had he insisted on Arlen continuing like that, long past his endurance? How had he managed to last that long? He had never been fucked like that before, he thought with amusement. His previous experiences were nothing compared to that. And even over the pain and exhaustion, it had been perfect.

"You can hear me?" Arlen repeated, still stunned.

"Yes," he said, then looked around. There were other creatures nearby, he realized, and he clutched Arlen for protection. Arlen looked up at the others.

"Stay back," he warned, and they backed off. Slightly.

Arlen helped him sit up and he winced as pain racked his body. He could still taste blood from where his tongue had tangled with Arlen's fangs and he was disappointed that they weren't able to kiss, but everything else between them was better than the best kiss so he wasn't too disappointed.

"Can you stand?"

"I think so," he said, and Arlen helped him to his feet cautiously, pausing as he gasped in pain. But he managed to stand. And realized he was completely naked and covered in the remnants of sex. He blushed and attempted to cover himself but the creatures around him had all seen. They must have seen everything, he thought in panic. Everything. His complete loss of control and everything that had happened between him and Arlen. He backed into the comfort of his creature and Arlen embraced him.

"You have nothing to be ashamed of," Arlen whispered to him. "You survived."

He blinked and realized it was still night. He was standing in the moonlight, surrounded by creatures of the night, embracing one of them, and he was alive. This had never happened before, he knew.

"Leave us," Arlen said to the others. "He needs to recover first."

Jarl didn't know what he meant by first, but he was grateful when the other creatures vanished into the night. He looked at Arlen shyly.

"I thought you gave up one me," he said.

Arlen chuckled. "You should have known I didn't."

"Then why wasn't I drawn here every night?"

"We can see the wall," he said. "The first night, I saw where you were and saw you get stopped. The two nights after that, there were four guards there so I knew there was no point bringing you out. I waited until they were gone and then summoned you."

"I didn't know you had that kind of control," Jarl said, thinking of the old timer's story of how it had been a week of attempts and then he had been left alone the rest of his life. And most people were only drawn out once and if they survived, it never happened again.

"We rarely use it," Arlen said. "If we don't get what we need immediately, we give up and try another. But I wanted you, and no one else, so I waited."

Jarl smiled, then shivered. It was cold in the night and he was naked and covered in cum.

"What do you need?" Arlen asked him, placing one hand under his chin and tilting it so that their eyes met. He had never imagined those large ebony eyes could look so concerned. It was definitely possible to read the creature's emotions.

Jarl pulled away slightly and looked down at himself.

"I need to bathe," he said. "And I need clothes. And I need to rest. What happened?"

"You found something to offer me that didn't kill you," Arlen said, and began leading him deeper in the woods. He followed. "Though I thought I was going to kill you until you saw the moon. I should be asking you what happened."

"It's beautiful," he said, looking at the pale sphere between the treetops. "When I looked at it, the music got quieter and everything made sense again."

"Can you still hear the music?" he asked curiously.

"It's still there," Jarl confirmed. "But it's faint. I can barely hear it. It's not driving me anymore."

"You've adapted," Arlen said with an indrawn breath, sounding awed.

They reached a small pond and Arlen gestured to the dark waters.

"This is all I can offer you to bathe. It's safe," he added, no doubt seeing Jarl's hesitation. "Nothing swims here. It's only water, and it's not deep. Here."

He stepped into the water and Jarl followed. Arlen led him to the center of the pond where the water reached his waist. It only reached the tops of Arlen's thighs and Jarl's gaze was drawn to his penis, just out of the water. Arlen followed his gaze and grinned.

"I had no idea this could do what we did," he said with a laugh. "Quite a versatile body part. We had always wondered why humans had such a vulnerable part."

Jarl began cleaning himself, then began cleaning Arlen as well, pulling him lower in the water so he could wash everything from the creature's beautiful body. Arlen helped once he realized what Jarl was doing, and soon they were both clean. They left the water and he realized they didn't have any towels or anything to dry off. Arlen went to a nearby bush, one of the ones with wide, flat leaves, and pulled off a leaf.

"Here," he said, handing Jarl the leaf before rubbing the leaf over his body the same way he would a towel. Cautiously, Jarl pressed the leaf on his skin. It was surprisingly soft and absorbed the water and soon he was dry. Arlen went to another tree and pulled down the kind of draping cloth he had been wearing earlier. How did cloth come from a plant? But it did, and Arlen dressed himself before pulling more cloth down and wrapping it around Jarl. He still felt naked, as the cloth didn't cover him as completely as clothes did, but he thought he would have the confidence to be seen by others now.

"We need to talk to the rest of the creatures before you can rest," Arlen said. "None of them will hurt you. None of them can hurt you, now. You're part of this planet."

"You said I was poison," he pointed out, and Arlen laughed.

"Your poison has been neutralized. How else were you able to use that leaf like that, or wear this cloth? The leaves are prickly to you humans, and this cloth would sting your skin if you didn't belong to this world. But everything on this planet is harmonized and you're part of us now, so everything here will adapt to your needs."

"But what happened?"

"I don't know," Arlen admitted. "We'll have to figure it out before we send you back."

"Back?" Jarl said in shock. "You can't send me back to the colony."

"Why not? We need you to teach the other humans what you did."

"They'll kill me," he said. "I survived the night. They'll assume I'm possessed, or I'm one of you posing as me, or something like that and they'll kill me."

Arlen studied him silently. "We need the other humans to learn from you," he said slowly, then sighed. "Maybe the others will know what to do. I won't let you be killed and you seem quite certain of what will happen."

CHAPTER 8

The creatures were terrifying. Jarl remembered what the old timer had said about the creature he saw being like a nightmare and many of these creatures looked exactly like the nightmares that had haunted him all of his life until recently. Arlen had brought him to a large clearing and led him to the center, where an enormous creature crouched, and they had immediately been surrounded. Some of the creatures looked human, like the woman who had nearly lured him to her. They were coldly beautiful. Others were like nightmares. But the one in front of them, the one at the center of the clearing, was unlike anything he'd ever seen.

It almost looked like an enormous tree come to life, though it was only about fifteen feet tall, not nearly tall enough for a trunk as wide as it had. It had a face of sorts, with ebony eyes like the other creatures and a wide mouth he knew without asking was filled with fangs, but there wasn't really a nose and the face wasn't part of a head. It was part of the rest of the body. There weren't really legs, either. The trunk just seemed to end at the ground. There were arms, long and scraggly like branches. It really did look like a tree come to life and his fear was balanced by his curiosity. A good thing, because when he looked at the other creatures fear definitely won out. He was grateful for Arlen at his side because he knew his creature would keep him safe.

Arlen bowed to the tree-creature as they stopped in front of it and Jarl felt a pulse from the music in his mind indicating that he should do the same, so he obeyed and bowed. He felt another pulse asking his name.

"I'm Jahl," he said cautiously, not sure who was asking or who he was supposed to be talking to. There was an immediate murmur from the creatures and the tree's eyes widened. Was he not supposed to talk? He looked around and the other creatures were clearly surprised, but why? Was he not supposed to give his name?

He felt another pulse, asking if he understood, and he looked at Arlen.

"Am I supposed to be answering this?" he asked softly.

Arlen's lips curled. "If you can understand what is being asked, you should speak. It is our planet speaking to you. We can all hear her. She's testing if you can hear her."

"Oh," he said. "Yes, I understand."

Another pulse, this one tinged with excitement, asking what happened. He looked Arlen again, because he didn't know what to say.

"I don't know what happened," he said.

A pulse asking how he understood the voice right now and he shrugged.

"I hear music now," he said. "I can hear you through the notes."

The creatures murmured again and Arlen looked pleased. Clearly that was a good answer, though he wasn't sure why.

"You hear our music, child?" a deep voice asked, and he realized the tree was talking.

"Yes," he said cautiously.

"Have you ever heard it before?"

"When I dreamed under the moon, I heard it and I didn't have nightmares," he said. "And when I was driven to the woods, I heard it so loudly I couldn't hear anything else."

"He looked at the moon before he regained control," Arlen said. "Maybe the moon is the key. Jarl, you had never looked at the moon before that night, had you?"

"Not really," he said. "I'd seen it, of course, but never studied it."

"Do other humans ever look at the moon? Really look at it?"

"I don't know," he said. "It's only there at night and we hide during the night, but there are people who study it. I don't know why anyone else would look at it."

"You must return and teach the other humans to look at the moon," the tree instructed, and Jarl flinched.

"They'll kill me," he said, and Arlen place an arm around his shoulders.

"He doesn't think the other humans will accept him now," he said. "Because he survived. He seems certain of it."

"Won't they want to know how you survived so they can also survive?" the tree asked, puzzled.

"Maybe, but what can I tell them? If I say I've been with creatures they'll kill me. You're enemies. You're evil. You kill people. They'll think I'm evil, too, and they'll kill me."

"Then say you were lured into the woods but you looked at the moon and its light protected you," the tree suggested, and he considered. Would that work?

"I don't want him in danger," Arlen said, glancing at him. "Would you be in danger if you said that?"

"They might not believe me," he said slowly. "But they would have to. They would want to test it, though, and I don't know how they would. And what if it didn't work? What if the moon doesn't do anything? I'll be trapped there."

"You don't want to be with other humans?" the tree asked, and he paused. Did he? He thought about his people and for some reason, felt distinctly uneasy about going back there. It wasn't just that he would probably be killed. He might survive if he told them about the moon. But he would be surrounded. He wanted to be out at night now so he could look at the moon but that would make him a target. And he would never be able to leave again, so he would never see Arlen again. No, he didn't want to go back.

Arlen shrugged. "We can't stand being around groups of humans, either. Now that he hears our music, I'm sure they're poison to him as well."

"We still have to teach the other humans what to do," the tree said. "He has to return."

Jarl shivered. Would Arlen defend him and fight for him to stay? Arlen looked at him and he longed for him to stay on his side in this argument. He felt a pulse in his mind but it wasn't from the planet. Arlen's eyes widened, as did the tree's. The other creatures murmured as well.

"You can control our song," Arlen said in surprise. "You feel that strongly about going back?"

Jarl realized that the pulse must have been him communicating through the music. But was it enough? Would Arlen stay on his side? Arlen sighed.

"We can't make him go back if he doesn't want to," he said to the tree. "Besides, he's valuable. He's the only human who's ever adapted. We can't throw his life away."

"If he remains the only human who's ever adapted, then he's useless," the tree said. "He must go back, no matter what he wants."

The female creature who had approached him in the woods and then tried to lure him earlier in the night stepped forward and Jarl flinched, drawing closer to Arlen.

"We can compel him to go back," she said. "If he hears us now, he has no choice. We can drive him back just as we drew him here."

"No," Arlen said, wrapping an arm around Jarl. "We're not doing this against his will."

The female bared her teeth, the fangs flashing in the moonlight.

"The elder is right," she said. "He has to go back. If he doesn't agree, I say we make him."

Jarl shivered and looked at Arlen, who looked angry.

"It's not your choice," he said in a low voice. "He's my intended. I decide what happens to him. If you had your way, he wouldn't be here at all. You tried to take him from me."

"He offered himself to me," she said with a sniff. "Who was I to stop him?"

"They can't control who they offer themselves to, you know that," Arlen snapped. "You made sure he saw you first. If I hadn't gotten his attention so quickly, he would be dead."

Jarl shivered. Was that true? He had been so sure that he would be drawn straight to Arlen. Was it really true that he would have offered himself to any creature he saw? He had tried to offer himself to her, he considered. He had offered her his flesh. Would he have been eaten if she had her way? Had she wanted to eat him? Arlen put his hand on Jarl's shoulder and met his eyes.

"But you do have to return, Jarl," he said. "Please."

Jarl was silent. Apparently they could compel him to return and while Arlen didn't want to use that option, the others might do it without his permission. He was only one creature, after all, and they were all determined to drive him back to the humans. And Arlen wanted him to return, too, so maybe he would eventually side with the others. His heart clenched. He had given Arlen his heart and body and now Arlen didn't want him?

"Let me talk to him in private," Arlen said, looking at the others. "He'll return, but I need to talk to him first."

Arlen took his hand and led him to the edge of the clearing. The creatures parted for them and he shivered as he walked through them. They were terrifying. He didn't want to go back to the colony but he also didn't want to live here with them. He wanted to live with Arlen and Arlen only.

As soon as they were in private, Arlen sat down and pulled him to sit next to him.

"Do you still think they'll kill you if you tell them about the moon, Jarl?" he asked quietly.

"That's not why I don't want to go back," he said, unsure how to explain.

"Then why?"

Jarl shut his eyes, unsure what to say. How could Arlen not understand the reason? Had he been numb while feeding on him? Did he really have no idea what Jarl had offered him?

"I offered you my heart," he said slowly, opening his eyes. "And now you're refusing it."

"You offered me your body, too, and taking that nearly killed you," Arlen pointed out. "Only the moon stopped you from giving yourself to me until you died."

"That might be true," he admitted, because it was almost certainly true. "But giving you my heart didn't hurt at all, or drain me, and it wouldn't have killed me."

Arlen was silent, then reached out and place his hand on Jarl's heart.

"I can still feel it," he said. "You're still offering yourself to me. But the music isn't driving you anymore. Why are you still offering yourself?"

"Don't you have love?" Jarl asked, exasperated that he still wasn't understanding. "Don't you know what it means to give someone your heart?"

"Love?" he repeated, caressing Jarl's chest through the draping cloth. "Is that what that delicious feeling was? No, we don't have it. What does it mean?"

"It... it means I love you," Jarl said with a blush, not knowing how else to explain it and incredibly uncomfortable to say it. He hadn't loved Arlen. He tolerated Arlen, maybe it had even moved to friendship, he could admit, but until the siren's song blasted through all his inhibitions, he hadn't realized it was love. The planet's music had skipped through all of the preliminary emotions and jumped straight to the most extreme and that was what he had offered.

"It felt strange," Arlen mused. "Like a connection between us, almost like the connection between me and this planet. Like we belonged together in some way, like you were trying to tie our minds together."

"That's love," Jarl said. "When you want to be with someone, when you never want to leave them. When they make up your world. I don't know why I feel that way about you but I do. I don't want to leave you."

"Then it's not the humans you're afraid of," he said in surprise.

"It is," Jarl said. "They won't ever allow me out again. Even if I convince them about the moon, even if that works, they'll never allow me to leave the colony. I'll never see you again. Don't you care about that? I thought you cared about me. I'm intended for you, after all."

"I do feel very… possessive of you," Arlen considered. "I don't want anyone to part us. You amuse me. I enjoy talking to you. I would like to see you every day for the rest of our lives. Is that also love?"

"Yes," Jarl said. "So please don't make me go back."

"Love is a complicated thing," Arlen said, and Jarl couldn't help but laugh.

"Humans have never understood it," he said. "There's almost no point trying. It just happens and you can't fight it."

"And you weren't hurt when you offered me your love," Arlen said thoughtfully. "Just when you offered me your body?"

"Yes," he said. "For me, love means sharing bodies, too."

"Is that true for everyone? Or can some people share love without bodies? Perhaps we can teach other humans to love us and we could feed safely," he said, clearly deep in thought. "How did I make you love me?"

Jarl blushed. "I don't know. As I said, it's complicated."

Arlen seemed to want a more complete answer and he sighed, trying to figure out why he had fallen for the creature.

"Well, you're very beautiful," he started, because that was the first thing that had drawn him. "Beauty is important, but everyone has their own standards of beauty. And you're kind. You helped me. And I suppose you amuse me, too. I liked talking to you and getting to know you. I wasn't in love with you, though. We were friends, I guess. But then that music filled me and I suddenly wanted you. I loved you. I don't know how it happened so quickly."

Arlen sighed. "We can try similar approaches with other humans, but we only have the chance for extended interactions once a year. In the meantime, you need to return. I don't want you to return, but you need to."

Jarl looked away and Arlen placed his hand on his heart again.

"I feel the way you do, Jarl," he said in a soft voice. "I love you. I will see you again. I will not let the humans keep you from me, even if I have to sneak into your colony in the dead of night when they aren't expecting it."

Jarl started in surprise. "Can you do that?"

"If I wanted, yes," he said, and Jarl licked his lips nervously. They had all assumed the colony was completely safe. It was why no one in the colony wore a mask, why they were able to sleep without fear for the most part. They had nightmares and some were drawn to the woods, but most slept soundly and he had never thought they were in danger of being overrun by the creatures. But if Arlen could get in, then perhaps he wouldn't be as trapped as he feared. He shut his eyes.

"Fine," he whispered. "If you want me to go, I will. I'll tell them to study the moon, to really look at it. I'll try to help the other humans become part of this world. But you can't leave me there forever. You have to come back."

Arlen leaned forward and kissed him sweetly, just their lips pressing against each other. Something fluttered in his belly and if his body weren't so incredibly sore, he might have pushed for more. But just the thought of sex made his body clench in pain. It would be a long time before he recovered from that. He wondered if any doctors would try to examine him after he returned. If so, they would almost certainly see his injuries and be able to guess what had caused them. He would be accused of sleeping with a creature and he would almost certainly be killed. There was so much risk in this but he would do it, because Arlen was asking him. He could feel encouragement from the music in his mind and knew that the planet wanted it as well but all he cared about was Arlen. Nothing else mattered.

"Thank you, Jarl," Arlen said, stroking his cheek as they broke apart. "Now you should rest. I'll carry you back to the edge of the woods and when you wake up, you can return to the colony."

"Will you be here when I wake up?"

"No," he said sadly. "It's too dangerous for us to be near here when the sun has risen, and you must wait until the sun is up to return."

"Will you guard me while I sleep?"

The corners of Arlen's lips curved. "Of course."

They stood up and then Arlen scooped him up, his larger frame easily able to carry the smaller Jarl. Arlen bent and kissed his forehead, and Jarl let his eyes drift shut. He was barely aware of being carried, barely aware of being laid down somewhere. He felt safe and secure and for the first time, his dreams weren't marred by any negative emotion. Even when he had dreamed under the moon and only remembered the melody, his dreams hadn't been positive. This time, they were, and it was the strangest thing he had ever experienced to fall into a slumber where he actually felt good. When he woke, he was alone and naked once again.

CHAPTER 9

Something prodded him and Jarl opened his eyes, wondering why he was naked again and what was happening. Someone was looking at him and when he opened his eyes, the figure cried out in shock and fell backwards. It was a human from the colony. Jarl sat up and looked around. Other humans were coming at his cry and they were staring at Jarl in absolute astonishment.

"You're alive," one of them muttered, and he realized who they were.

When the sun was safely in the sky, a patrol was set out to collect the bodies of those who had been drawn to the woods. They usually had some idea which way the bodies went and it didn't take long to collect them. Jarl had been on that patrol many times. It was one of the worst jobs and as such, everyone had to do it occasionally. The bodies were usually quite gruesome. Even the ones that looked untouched had that liquid coming from their ears that chilled him. If he had found one of those bodies alive, he would have been shocked as well.

The one who found him knelt beside him and stared into his eyes. "Are you okay? Do you know where you are?"

"I'm in the woods," he said, a little shaky because the man was looking at him warily and without the warmth he had hoped for. "I survived," he added, hoping that would help. "I was drawn here and then I-"

"Shush," the man said before he could tell him about the moon, and he obeyed. "Let's get you back. Evan, give me your jacket or something. What do we have to cover him?"

Evan grumbled but took off his jacket and handed it to Jarl.

"He must have snuck out this morning," he said skeptically. "He couldn't have been out last night."

"Why would anyone sneak out in the morning?" the first man asked in annoyance. Jarl didn't know him, though he was familiar. Everyone in the colony was familiar to some degree since he passed them in the streets and worked beside a variety of people. He had probably worked with this man at some point, but hadn't bothered to get to know him. Since their jobs rotated so frequently, he rarely got to know the people he worked with. Only the other harvesters were exceptions, because their jobs were permanent.

He helped Jarl stand up and he winced. His whole body ached but he couldn't show it. Why had Arlen stripped him? Now his injuries were obvious to anyone looking. Luckily, no one was looking and one of the woman approached with a blanket for him to wrap around himself. The man kicked the ground nearby and he saw the torn remnants of his pajamas. Arlen must have retrieved them, but there were in no shape to wear.

"A creature must have attacked you," he said slowly. "Why didn't it kill you?"

"I looked at the moon, and it felt like the moonlight protected me," he said. "The creature left."

"The moon?" the man repeated in a disbelieving voice, but the woman looked impressed.

"The moon is what keeps them back during the peace," she said. "You just looked at the moon and you were safe?"

"I really looked at it," he said, unsure how to explain what had happened. "It was like I felt the moon in my soul."

The others looked at each other nervously, even the woman, and he wondered if that was too much.

"We'll get you back," the man said. "What's your name?"

"Jarl," he said, and the man blinked in surprise.

"You're the harvester," he said, and Jarl nodded. He grinned. "Praise Earth. The president and the old timers were frantic when it was discovered you were gone. They were hoping you were just hiding somewhere but we were sent to check for you out here anyway. Four others escaped last night. It was a bad night. Do you think any of them survived?"

"I hope so," he said, though his heart sank as he thought of the female creature. Had she left to find another victim? If any of the others had survived, he would have been told. They had all been killed. The creatures had killed all of them, and then had the gall to stand around him and talk about sending him back to the humans to die. He might love Arlen, but he despised the rest of them.

They headed back and Jarl's body continued to ache. He had to pause at several points and worried what people would think. He would definitely be examined, he knew, and dreaded it. What was he supposed to say? What did he look like? What would people think?

As soon as they entered the colony gates, they were flooded by people and in minutes, the president and all of the old timers were at his side shouting questions at him. He shied away, unsure what to say and who to answer. There was just too much chaos. The president seemed to recognize how overwhelmed he felt and instructed the people escorting him to bring him to his house. She followed him in and the man helped him into his bed, pulling the blanket over him before taking the jacket back. The president and two old timers stood in his room, looking down at him in relief.

"What happened, Jarl?" asked the old timer who trained him, Doss.

"I was drawn to the woods and a creature appeared, but I looked at the moon and it felt like the moonlight protected me," he said, still not entirely sure how to explain.

"You looked at the moon?" the president asked, puzzled. She looked at the old timers. "What would the moon have to do with anything?"

"Maybe there's some lingering power from the peace," Doss considered. "We know the moon is responsible for calming the creatures so we can leave during the peace. Maybe there was some of that energy left."

"I'll consult with the astronomers," she said, then looked back at Jarl. "You're injured. Were you attacked?"

"I don't know," he said, and she sighed.

"We'll get someone to look at you. Try to recover. We'll have guards on you from now on, so don't worry. We'll never let you get lured again."

He inwardly winced. That was exactly what he didn't want. But there was nothing he could do about it so he just nodded and they filed out. He shut his eyes. He did feel weak, and slightly nauseous. It wasn't anything physical, he thought, but something was making him queasy. A doctor entered and the feeling strengthened, but he was too worried now about the exam to worry about a minor belly upset.

The doctor asked him what happened in a quiet voice and he repeated his story, then the doctor removed the blanket and his eyes widened.

"You were attacked," he said, and Jarl looked down at himself. His arms were bruised where Arlen must have grabbed him, and the skin over his heart was bruised as well. As were his sides and legs, he realized. No wonder he ached so badly. He hadn't realized it when they were making love, but Arlen had been brutal to him. He had invited it, he admitted. He had needed it. He hoped that when they did it again, it wouldn't be so violent, and then he flushed. Would they do it again? He would have to get out of this colony first. Even if Arlen managed to sneak in, there was no way he was going to sleep with a creature here.

"Turn over," the doctor said, and he winced but obeyed. He felt the doctor's hands run over him, pausing on his hips. "Were you with someone last night?" he asked.

"I don't know," Jarl said, feeling awkward. It was probably clear what had happened.

"Who were you with?" the doctor asked. "They might be in danger."

He helped Jarl roll over and he puzzled. "What do you mean?"

"You must have been with them when you were drawn, or it was right after," the doctor said. "They might have been drawn as well. We lost four last night. Who were you with?"

Jarl's eyes widened. The doctor thought he had been with someone before he was lured into the woods. He thought that damage was from a human. He had to bite back his relief.

"Who died?" he asked. This was good, but who could he say? Should he say someone who died, or pretend it was someone else and just not name them?

"Another harvester," the doctor said sadly, and Jarl gasped. "It was almost a very bad night for our colony. We almost lost two of you."

"Who?" Jarl asked, heart pounding loudly. There were only twelve of them and he knew them better than anyone else. He squabbled with them sometimes and he and Terran had a friendly rivalry that sometimes spilled into genuine anger, but they were all dear to him. The doctor sighed.

"Kandor. Second longest route. We would have been lost if both of you had been killed."

Jarl couldn't move, couldn't think. He had just seen Kandor. They had talked just yesterday. Kandor had asked him about what it was like to be drawn to the woods, and he had avoided answering. And now Kandor had been drawn to the woods and killed. He shut his eyes and felt a tear streak down his cheek.

He imagined the cruel female creature, or one of the creatures who looked like a nightmare, finding his beloved friend. He imagined Kandor offering his flesh the way Jarl had tried to do at first. He had been driven to offer himself and been desperate to feed Arlen. Had Kandor felt the same? Had he felt completion when he was eaten alive? Jarl sobbed, turning in the bed to curl into a ball. Kandor was gone, eaten by the very creatures who had spoken to him and watched him and left him alive. He couldn't bear it.

The doctor patted his shoulder. "I'm sorry, Jarl."

"Did... did you find his body? What happened to him?"

"Do you really want to know?" he asked softly.

"Yes," Jarl whispered.

"He was eaten," the doctor said. "I'm sorry."

Jarl let out another sob and the doctor patted him again. "Get some rest," he said gently. "I'll be back in a little with some cream that will help those bruises, but the main thing you need is sleep."

"I can't sleep," he said, thinking of the nightmares that would surely accompany it. He had avoided nightmares last night but now, with thoughts of Kandor so fresh in his mind, he knew his dreams would be excruciating.

"The dreams are better during the day," the doctor said soothingly. "And you need rest. At least close your eyes."

Jarl nodded and the doctor left, promising to return soon. Once he was alone, Jarl lay on his back and felt the gentle hum of the melody in his mind. He hated it. That melody had destroyed his friend. That melody had lured his friend out of safety into the jaws of a monster. There had to be some way to rid himself of that melody. He tried to think of other music that might drown it out, playing through the hymns and marches of the colony as loudly as he could in his mind, but the melody always remained, just under the surface.

There was nothing he could do to rid himself of it and finally he let out a cry of rage and sorrow and sat up, clutching his head. He couldn't do this. He couldn't bear the thought that he had survived but everyone else had died. Why was he the only survivor? How was he any better than his friend?

There was a pulse in the music and he felt reassurance. He rejected it, but the pulse came again, stronger, forcing his thoughts to quiet. He took a deep breath, almost against his will, and felt calm spread through him. If he taught the humans, then no one would ever die like that again. The message washed over him. That was his duty. To prevent more deaths. But what did it matter when Kandor was already dead?

The door opened and the doctor came in, seeming surprised that Jarl was sitting up. He clucked his tongue sympathetically and laid out a few jars before slathering thick cream on his bruises. They started healing immediately but the pain lingered, and the pain in his heart would never go away. He finally lay down and shut his eyes, just wanting to escape, even if it was into nightmares.

CHAPTER 10

Days and nights passed in a blur as he recovered from the shock of what had happened. He continued to feel nauseous but when he brought it up with the doctor, he hadn't found anything to cause the feeling. He suggested, gently, that it might be because he was in mourning.

Everyone treated him very gently and Doss stopped by every day. He didn't leave his house, but a variety of people came to talk to him. The people who studied the moon quizzed him repeatedly but he wasn't sure what to say except that you had to really look at the moon. Not analyze it through a telescope, as they did, but look at it in the sky and appreciate its beauty. They scoffed, saying there was no point looking at it with plain vision when the telescopes produced such clarity. Others came, too, and he urged them to look at the moon, but he wasn't sure anyone was listening. He felt helpless. His body had recovered but he still felt weak and more than anything else, he missed Arlen.

A week passed before he felt a pull one night. There were guards stationed at his door, he knew, to keep the night from taking him a second time, so he went to the window. The moon was overhead and he let out a sigh of admiration. He sat down and stared up at it. Were any of the others humans looking at it right now? Had any of them listened to him? Or were they all huddled in their homes, terrified of the wind that was starting to pick up and that would inevitably bring some of them into the woods to their deaths? He gazed at the moon and felt the melody in his mind grow a little louder.

He shut his eyes. He hadn't been having nightmares, at least not the usual nightmares. He was still wracked with grief over Kandor's death and the minutes before and after he fell asleep were filled with guilt and anger, but the sleep itself was neutral. As he leaned his head on his arms in the window under the light of the moon, he felt peace finally come over him. He sighed and relaxed into a deep, pleasant sleep, the kind of sleep the original colonists must have had. The kind of sleep that must have been possible on Earth.

When he woke, there was a commotion outside. For the first time since he had returned from the woods, he dressed and opened his door. The guard outside looked excited and without a word, brought him to the center of the commotion. He blanched as he saw a young woman bleeding in the center of the crowd. Her right arm and part of her shoulder had been bitten off and he recognized the signs of feeding left by the creatures. But then he blinked. She had been eaten but she was here, alive. Her arm was gone and she was covered in blood and other scratches, but she was alive. Her eyes met his and he recognized her as the woman who had helped him when he was first discovered in the woods. A weak smile crossed her lips and he pushed up to her. Everyone let him through. The doctors were already at her side and the president was there as well, but she gestured for Jarl to come closer and he knelt by the bleeding figure.

"I did what you said," she whispered. "When the creature began eating me, I looked at the moon. It was so beautiful. So peaceful. Nothing hurt when I looked at the moon. The creature left and they found me this morning."

"The moon?" the president asked, sounding urgent. "You're sure it was the moon?"

Jarl's eyes filled with tears. It had worked. Someone else had been spared.

"It was the moon," she said weakly, then fell back, unconscious.

Jarl looked at the damage that had been done and the frantic way the doctors were trying to help her and realized she probably wouldn't survive. But she had survived the night, and that was what mattered. They would listen to him now, and they had a chance of survival. The president stood and Jarl was escorted into the capital behind her, the old timers at his side. Jarl was pushed into one of the chairs and the others sat as well, then the guards left. When it was only him, the president, and the old timers, she leaned towards him intently.

"Others have been looking at the moon since you returned," she said. "Why did it work for her and no one else?"

"You have to really look at the moon," he said, as he had said before. "I don't know how to explain it. You look at the moon and realize how beautiful it is, and then everything is calm. I didn't even have nightmares after I looked at the moon."

"Does it have to be at the attack itself?" she asked. "It's a lot to ask someone to remember to look at the moon when they're being eaten."

"You can look at the moon and see its beauty anytime, but I think you have to do it during the attack as well," he said. After all, it was only when he looked at the moon that he had snapped out of the siren's call of offering himself to Arlen.

"We can train people," Doss said, sounding excited. "We can teach them to look at the moon so that it's instinct when they're attacked."

"No one has ever survived before," another old timer said in awe. "And now two have. Is it really as simple as the moon?"

"There has to be something else going on," said the oldest old timer with a scowl. "It's still close to the peace. I doubt this will continue to happen as we get into the rest of the year."

"We should still try," Doss snapped. "It's the first hope we've ever had on this damn planet."

"This planet has laid traps before," the oldest one said bitterly.

Her great-grandmother had been one of the original colonists and she often reminded them of it. She had known her grandmother, the first generation of people raised entirely on this planet. She remembered the stories about when the planet had turned on them and was frequently telling them to the children so they wouldn't be forgotten. She was over a hundred now but sharp as ever, and the fact that she had never been called to her death meant she was revered over everyone else here. All of the old timers were honored, but she was a good twenty years older than the second oldest of them and she never let anyone forget it. As far as Jarl was concerned, she would always be a part of the colony.

"Jarl and Issa survived," Doss emphasized. "How is that a trap?"

"Maybe they're being prepared for something worse later," she said darkly, and Jarl shivered. "Maybe they'll be called to the woods again someday, in weeks or months or years, and will face something far worse than being eaten."

"That won't happen," Jarl said, because if she convinced the others that he was always in danger, then he would never get back to the woods to see Arlen. And if she thought the planet was going to hurt him more, then there would be almost no way to convince them that the creatures weren't enemies. Or at least that Arlen wasn't an enemy. If this old timer convinced them that Jarl couldn't be trusted, then everything fell apart.

"Maybe we should train someone for both harvests," the president said slowly. "We need those plants and if they are just waiting to take Jarl next year when he's vulnerable, then we'll lose that harvest."

Jarl's eyes widened. That was bad. He had counted on being able to go alone because then, even if he hadn't seen Arlen in the year until the next peace, at least he would have five days with him.

"I'm not sure we have two people ready to take on both of our long harvests," Doss said grimly. "I'll start training them at once, of course. We can cover Kandor's harvest but you know how difficult Jarl's is."

"I can still go," he said quickly. "I won't fail. The creatures can't hurt us then. I'll be able to bring the pods back safely. I have every year since I took the harvest. You can trust me."

The president looked at Doss, who shrugged. "I'll prepare someone, but it is safest to let him do it. Or we could send them out together so that at least one makes it back."

"That would doom both of them to death," the oldest one said. "If the planet has sentenced Jarl to a darker fate, then anyone with him would be in danger."

"I haven't been sentenced to anything," Jarl protested. This conversation was not going well. "I survived, and nothing else will happen to me. Others can survive, too."

There was a knock at the door and one of the guards approached. "Issa died," he said simply. "Blood loss."

The president nodded and the guard left.

"You survived," the president said. "And she survived at first, but we can't expect people to remember to look at the moon, especially if they have to look at the moon a certain way. Maybe they'll survive the night, like Issa did. But she still died."

"We have to try," Jarl said, not knowing what else to do. The president sighed.

"All right. We'll talk to people and try to make them look at the moon. What do you have to do? Look at the moon and think it's beautiful?"

"You can't just think it, you have to feel it," Jarl said. "But it is beautiful. It isn't hard to do. I had never looked at the moon before, not really. When you do look at it, it's hard not to think it's beautiful."

"I'm not sure I've ever looked at the moon," the president said thoughtfully. "Perhaps I'll try tonight."

Jarl smiled, grateful, and then the others let him leave for the day. A week had passed so he would be back to regular work, he knew. A week was all they ever gave people, no matter the cause. He was just grateful they had given him the entire week because he knew most people received far less when someone close to them died. He didn't mind the work, though, he thought as he was brought to the kitchens were he was most of the time. It would help keep his mind of Arlen.

He wondered as he worked, though. Had Arlen fed on other humans? Was he feeding on them even now? He wouldn't be able to help it; Jarl understood that now. Arlen had been as helpless in feeding on him as Jarl was in offering himself. If Jarl had only offered his heart, he would have been fine, he thought with a blush. There had been no problems with that. It was only because he was also attracted to Arlen and had wanted to give his body that there was a problem.

He wondered if other humans could learn to love the creatures. They only had five days a year when they could interact with the creatures safely, but that had been enough time to win his heart. He hoped the creatures tried again next year. Would he still be in this colony next year? He put his hand over his belly and thought of the nausea that never quite went away, and the fear and angst he felt around all of these disbelieving people. He hoped he wasn't here, but he didn't want to be with the creatures, either. He might be part of this world now and he heard the music clearly in the back of his mind, but he was still afraid of it.

Everyone was glad to have Jarl back. It seemed like everyone in the colony knew him now and held him in awe. He supposed he would have been impressed if someone else had survived, so he tried to be as humble as possible when dealing with people. His coworkers were more casual with him than anyone else and he was glad. He frequently worked with the same people and wouldn't be able to stand it if they treated him with the reverence some people had. Almost everyone in the colony had a main job that they did three weeks of the month and then they alternated between the necessary but less desirable jobs the other week. Jarl and the other harvesters were a little different because half of the year was divided between their normal work and training for the harvest, but he still worked that schedule and was glad to be back with people he knew. It started to reduce the sting of losing Kandor.

He told everyone about the moon, of course, and they all listened. He suspected most of them would try it. They trusted him because they'd worked with him for years, unlike the others who barely knew him. And one of them, Ender, seemed especially interested. After several days, he approached Jarl shyly. At his request, Jarl went out with him that night, safe in the heart of the colony where the wind wouldn't claim them and the guards would have plenty of time to stop them if it did. It was in one of the grassy areas and Jarl laid down in the grass the way Arlen had once, cradling his head in his hands and missing the creature. Ender, after a moment, did the same. The moon was almost directly overhead and Jarl sighed in awe at the sight. It soothed him as nothing else did.

"It really is beautiful," Ender said. "You're right. I never have looked at it before. It looks like two mice chasing each other, doesn't it?"

"Two rabbits," Jarl said absently, then laughed. "I suppose it doesn't matter, does it? They're not real."

"I can see rabbits," Ender said consideringly. "They do seem to have ears. I hadn't noticed. So this is what you saw when you were outside?"

"Yes," Jarl said, and realized Ender was looking at him, not the moon.

"You're beautiful, too," Ender said in a husky voice, and Jarl blushed. He sat up and looked away, and Ender sat up too and placed his hand over Jarl's. "I'm sorry. You just look so peaceful in the moonlight. I know you still miss him."

Everyone had assumed he and Kandor had a much deeper relationship than they had but Jarl had never corrected them. It helped explain his injuries and his death had struck him as deeply as it would have if they had been together. And to be honest, he had considered it on many occasions. Sometimes he saw Kandor looking at him, and sometimes he looked back the same way. But they had never done anything and he regretted it deeply now.

"I suppose everyone dies eventually," he said. "I just wish he hadn't died like that. Or on that night."

The timing upset him more than anything else. While Jarl

was surviving, Kandor wasn't. What made Jarl so much better than his best friend? Why had the creatures spared him and not his friend? Why had Arlen approached him in a friendly manner and earned his trust, allowing him to survive, but no one had approached Kandor? The creatures had exactly the same opportunity with Kandor, with all of the harvesters, really. Most harvesters were only out one or two nights, he supposed, but Kandor was out four nights the same as Jarl. Why was Arlen the only creature willing to approach a human like that?

"I'm glad you survived," Ender said, squeezing his hand and scooting closer. "Otherwise you wouldn't be here right now."

Jarl looked over at him and realized what he was intending. He considered refusing, but felt almost a sense of helplessness. He was alone, without Arlen, among these humans that he no longer felt any true connection with. Maybe if he let this happen, he would feel like they were his people again.

He leaned towards Ender and their lips locked in a kiss. He remembered kissing Arlen and his fangs, but Ender was all sweetness under his tongue and he found himself pulling Ender closer, drawing him in, eager for this sensation he had missed. Ender wrapped his arms around him and he melted against him, feeling a need stirring inside him.

He wanted to offer himself to Ender but the man wouldn't understand and wouldn't be able to accept what he was offering. He needed Arlen to satisfy the craving to offer himself. Would Arlen even be able to feed on him now that he was part of the planet? Well, everything had to feed, he considered. Arlen would still need to feed, and he could offer himself in place of drawing in innocent humans. Maybe Arlen wouldn't be able to feed on anyone else, he thought. While he didn't want Arlen to starve, that thought pleased him. He would be Arlen's only, just as Arlen was the only one in his heart.

"Come home with me," Ender said, though he made it a question instead of a command.

Should he? Part of him wanted to go with Ender and forget his worries and fears in a moment of bliss, but would it be betraying Arlen? Did it matter if he betrayed Arlen? Arlen wasn't here, after all, and might never be here.

"Not yet," he whispered. "I'm not ready yet. Ask me again in a few weeks."

Ender smiled and kissed him again, and he sunk into the sensation. When they finally pulled apart, Ender's eyes were dazed with pleasure but he nodded.

"I will ask you," he promised. "And I'll hope for a different answer."

They laid back down and gazed at the moon for a while, holding hands but otherwise not touching. They didn't talk, either, too comforted by the sight of the glowing orb watching over them. Finally, when the moon moved out of view behind the tall buildings of the colony, they stood up. Ender kissed him one last time, sweetly, and they parted ways.

CHAPTER 11

There was another survivor the next morning, and as he was brought into the colony with fanfare, Jarl again pushed to the front and stared. The man was wrapped in a blanket the same way Jarl had been after the attack and he couldn't see the damage. He was limping and appeared to be in pain, but he was walking on his own and there were no missing limbs that he could see. He also wasn't immediately swarmed by doctors. There was only a single doctor, the same doctor that had helped Jarl and was the head doctor of the colony every week except his work week. Even then, he was on call. The president was there, of course, and the old timers gathered quickly. But while before they had included Jarl in their discussions of the survivor, this time they didn't and he hoped that wasn't a bad sign.

He returned to his day, wondering how the survivor was doing and how he had been hurt. And he considered. The night Issa had survived, he had gotten up and looked at the moon, and she had also looked at the moon. Last night, he had been looking at the moon most of the night. Was he doing something? He knew others had to be looking at the moon at this point, but no one else was surviving. Did he have to be looking at the moon at the same time as them? There was no real way to tell because he couldn't ask the people who died if they had managed to look at the moon. He could only ask the survivors and he strongly suspected the man had been looking at the moon at the same time Jarl was looking at it. But why?

That night, he spent hours gazing at the moon before going to bed. In the morning, there was a survivor. The next night, he stayed away from the window. There were no survivors. He knew he should test it more thoroughly but if him looking at the moon was saving lives, he needed to keep doing it. So he began spending at least three hours each night just staring at the moon, and survivors became regular. The longer he looked at the moon, the healthier they were when they returned. On the night when he only remembered to look at the moon right before it sank, the woman had survived but died of her wounds the way Issa had. He was definitely doing something to impact their survival, but what? And why?

Weeks passed, months passed, and he wondered where Arlen was. He had promised to find Jarl even if he had to come to the colony at night, but he hadn't shown up and Jarl was starting to miss him fiercely. Ender had asked him again, as he had expected, and he had agreed, not knowing what else to do. They often went to look at the moon together but sometimes Jarl had to wait until after they'd made love to go to the window and stare at the moon. Ender noticed how frequently he looked at the moon and commented on it once, but he had managed to avoid the topic.

Six months passed since the peace when he had met Arlen and Doss called him and all of the harvesters for the first meeting of their training. There were several youngsters with them to learn the routes in case something happened, but it seemed that they were going to allow Jarl to take his path as usual even if they were starting to train a replacement. It wasn't a bad idea. They probably should have someone ready for all of the paths just in case.

He wondered if he would see Arlen during the next peace. He ached for the creature and felt completely abandoned here. The nausea had never gone away, though he had stopped complaining about it. He accepted it. He had finally remembered that humans were like poison to the planet and he was likely responding to that. At times it was hard to remember that he was connected to the planet, since he didn't feel any different except the song in his mind and the queasiness in his belly. Maybe the planet had abandoned him the same way Arlen had, and he would be doomed to live here forever.

The first day of training went well. He was sore, as he always was. They started slow with the training and Jarl had kept himself in shape the past six months, as he always did, but they needed to be in peak physical shape for the harvest and it was hard work getting there. He went to the window as he always did, knowing he needed to look at the moon for there to be survivors. Getting drawn into the woods was no longer a death sentence and people were becoming curious about it, not frightened. He needed to do his part to protect them.

"Did you miss me?" a deep voice said, and he jumped. He whirled, breath catching.

The tall, powerful shape was unmistakable and for a moment fear crashed over him at the sight of a creature so close, but this was Arlen. He wouldn't hurt him. Couldn't hurt him. He stood up slowly, turning to face Arlen. Arlen grinned and he pushed aside his fear at the sight of those fangs. Without another thought, he rushed the creature and flung himself into his arms, embracing him tightly. Arlen was here. Finally, after months and months of waiting and fearing and missing him, Arlen was here. He pulled back and slammed his fist into Arlen's chest.

"Where have you been?" he cried, though he kept his voice down as he didn't want anyone to hear.

"It's not easy to get in," Arlen said. "This is the first time I've been able, but I've been trying for quite a while."

"But you're safe, aren't you?" Jarl asked, fear clenching his throat.

"As safe as I'll ever be in a human colony," he said with a laugh. "I suppose as safe as you were with me before you became part of our planet."

"You're not safe, then," Jarl said. "You shouldn't be here if you're in danger."

"Do you want me to leave?" Arlen asked, his lips curling as Jarl shook his head quickly.

"Don't ever leave," he said, pulling Arlen into another hug. "How long can you stay?"

"Perhaps an hour, perhaps less," he said. "The moon is strong tonight and I'm protected, but I can't risk too much. Still, I promised to visit you."

"Thank you," he whispered. "I've needed you."

"You've found someone to replace me," Arlen said, and Jarl blushed.

"How do you know about that?"

"You're connected to our planet," Arlen said with a chuckle. "And you look at the moon every night. You're connected to the moon when you do that and if I'm looking at the moon at the same time as you, I can catch glimpses of how you're doing."

He blushed, feeling as if his privacy had been deeply invaded. He had felt the same when he realized Arlen was based on his dreams. The planet had little regard for privacy.

"No one else can do it," Arlen added quickly, no doubt sensing his embarrassment and the sense of violation he felt. "You're intended for me, so I'm connected to you. And also..."

His voice faded and he place a hand over Jarl's heart, which skipped a beat. "We're connected by more, now. I didn't realize knowing you were with someone else would make me so angry, but it has. Is that part of love?"

"That's jealousy," Jarl said with a blush. So Arlen was jealous of Ender? Well, maybe if Arlen had been at his side all this time, he wouldn't have turned to Ender. But he couldn't blame Arlen. He didn't want his creature putting himself in danger.

"Humans are surviving now," Jarl said. "I've done what you wanted."

"They're surviving, but not on their own," Arlen said slowly. "You realize you're the one doing it, don't you?"

Jarl looked away. "I suspected. They only survive when I'm looking at the moon. But I can't stay here any longer. I want to be with you. I don't ever want to leave you again."

"Good, because I'm starving," Arlen said with a chuckle, his hand still over his heart. Without a word, Jarl offered his love to him and he could feel Arlen feeding on him. "No body this time?" he teased, and Jarl laughed.

"Not in the middle of the colony. You'll have to take me with you if you want more."

"I do want more," Arlen said as he drank in his love. "But you need to stay. You're doing good things, but we need more. You're still the only one who's adapted to this planet, though the others are learning to survive."

"The only time you can talk to us is during the peace, though," Jarl pointed out. "Are you going to try again next year?"

"We'll try," Arlen said. He shut his eyes. "This is far more delicious than anything I've ever fed on. Does it feel good to you?"

Jarl grinned. "It feels-"

There was a crash and a shot rang out. Arlen flinched backwards, the contact between them snapping abruptly. Jarl looked in shock to see Ender in the entrance to the room, holding a gun.

"No," he cried, then turned to see Arlen holding his side as the bullet fell from his body and the wound closed on its own. It was night; bullets couldn't hurt the creatures.

"Jarl, come here," Ender said in a low voice. "I'll protect you from that *thing*."

"Ender, you don't understand," Jarl said. He could hear his pulse in his ears, louder even than the song of the planet. What was he going to do? Others would hear the gun, he knew. Arlen needed to leave, now. He turned to Arlen.

"Get to safety. Don't come back. I'll see you at the peace," he said softly, so Ender wouldn't hear. Arlen darted to the window and vanished, and Jarl looked at Ender and wondered what he could possibly say.

"What was that creature doing here?" Ender demanded. "Why didn't it kill you? Why didn't it lure you? How did it get here?"

"Ender, I-"

"You made a deal with it, didn't you?" Ender asked, voice full of shock. "Is that why we're surviving now? You sold your soul to those demons and now they're sparing us?"

Jarl paused and considered. That was essentially what had happened, after all. Would it be bad to let Ender think that?

"You can't tell anyone," he said, trying to figure out how to turn this to his advantage. "You have to promise me. If the others know, they'll kill me and people will die again."

Ender lowered the gun that he still held in the air. "You really made a pact with that thing?"

"Please, Ender," he said. "Don't tell anyone. You can't."

Ender looked stunned and then he heard the door burst open. Why hadn't he heard the door when Ender entered? Ender came here often enough, but he had never given the man the key. Maybe he had left the door unlocked, he considered. That must have been it. People rarely locked their doors in the colony but he had been careful in case Arlen showed up. And the one night he did show up, Jarl had forgotten. He cursed himself, but couldn't let Ender see his anger.

Five guards rushed in and filled the room, clearly looking for the cause of the gunshot. They took Ender's gun but obviously didn't see him or Jarl as threats. The two of them were hustled out.

"What happened?" one of the guards asked them, and Jarl looked at Ender helplessly. Would he explain?

"It's my fault," Ender said after a long, soul-searching look at Jarl. "He was looking at the moon like he always does and I got frustrated he wasn't looking at me, and I fired to get his attention."

Jarl let out a breath and his tension faded.

"Why would you do such a thing?" the guard said, sounding more annoyed than angry. "We'll have to confiscate your gun for a week, and you'll need to attend a class on anger management. Should I put the two of you in couples counseling or can you work this out on your own?"

"We can work it out," Jarl said quickly, not wanting to have to go to counseling with Ender and potentially expose what had just happened. "There's nothing wrong with our relationship."

He looked at Ender meaningfully as he said that, hoping Ender understood. Their relationship would continue as it had been. Even though seeing Arlen had filled him desire for the creature and lessened what he felt for Ender, he would still take Ender to bed because he owed Ender now. He would be willing to offer his body in payment for his silence.

"Obviously something is wrong or he wouldn't be firing a gun to get your attention," the guard said, clearly disgruntled. "I'm taking your gun, too, Jarl. No chances."

Jarl went to his bedside and retrieved his gun, then handed it over. He wasn't surprised that the guard knew his name; it seemed like everyone in the colony knew him now. He wondered who the guard was going to tell about this. Hopefully no one except the people in charge of guns and whoever did the anger management. It was a fairly standard punishment. Jarl had even gone to anger management after getting into a fight with another harvester. Their colony was too small to allow feuds and anger to run wild, so it was strictly regulated. Ender would sit through a lecture for two hours and spend a few more hours practicing handling his anger in positive ways, and then he would be done. Jarl was relieved that there wouldn't be any other consequences, because he wasn't sure if Ender would tolerate anything else before saying what he had seen.

The guard started to hustle Ender away.

"Wait," Jarl said, and came to Ender's side. Very carefully, he embraced the man. Ender was at first stiff in his arms, then softened and hugged him back. "Thank you," he whispered.

"You'd better make it up to me," Ender whispered back with a hint of humor.

That was good, Jarl thought as they parted and grinned at each other. Ender didn't realize what had truly happened, that Jarl was in love with the creature. He thought he still had Jarl's heart and as long as that was true, he wouldn't say anything. Then the guards pulled Ender away and he was left alone in his room. He went to the window and looked out over the colony, wondering how Arlen had gotten in and hoping he got out safely. Then his eyes, almost inevitably, were drawn to the glowing moon and he felt happy as he hadn't since leaving Arlen's side six months ago.

CHAPTER 12

Despite Jarl's protests that he could handle his path alone during the harvest, Doss insisted that the girl who had been training with him should accompany him. Normally only one person went because of the danger but they didn't view the danger in the same way since people had begun surviving. The other paths would still have one person but Jarl's would have two, and he knew some of that was because of the oldest woman, who still feared that something would happen to Jarl and he wouldn't finish his harvest.

His heart sank as he and Keisha set out early in the first morning of the peace. He was a little tense as the entered the woods, since there was always the risk that the peace wouldn't come each year and while he wasn't in danger from the woods, she was. But nothing happened and they went quickly. They had to pause more often than he preferred, as she had never walked such a long distance over ground like this. It was quite a bit of an adjustment. The paths were clear and easy to follow, but they weren't roads like in the colony. Of course, Doss arranged for them to practice with fallen trees and rough terrain, but there was a big difference between practice and walking like this for five days. Walking with a mask also made a difference, he knew. In in the colony it barely made a difference but out here, the mask cut off his peripheral vision and always put him on edge, and he knew Keisha felt the same.

As the sun began to sink, he explained how to walk in the

dark, and when to put the goggles on. He usually went an hour after the sun fell before putting on the goggles because it was generally still light enough to get by and the goggles were bulky and made walking more difficult. As the sky darkened and he considered telling her to put them on, the path suddenly grew lighter and there was a familiar clopping sound. Surely Arlen wouldn't come to him with someone else here. They rounded a bend and he stopped with a gasp.

A crack rang through the night and he saw that Keisha had fired immediately and was crouched in a defensive position. The creature in front of them stared at them, unharmed. It wasn't Arlen, but it wasn't like the female who had threatened Jarl last year. This one looked as approachable as Arlen had and lifted his arms the same way Arlen had, as if to indicate peace.

He was quite handsome, though not nearly as perfect as Arlen. Jarl glanced at Keisha, whose eyes were wide in surprise at the sight of the creature. Was this creature drawn from her dreams and desires? He had to be, and he felt almost embarrassed to have such an intimate look into what she wanted.

"I mean you no harm," the creature said, and Keisha looked at Jarl fearfully.

"What do we do?" she hissed.

"Nothing," he said. "He can't hurt us right now. We continue."

"But there's a creature in our path," she said, clearly terrified.

"I saw one last year, and he didn't hurt me," Jarl said, and the girl's eyes narrowed.

"You what?"

"Yeah," he said. "He was friendly. He let me pass and even helped me."

"Creatures aren't friendly," she said, puzzled. But her fear was starting to pass. She straightened and lowered her gun, looking at the creature. "Are you friendly?"

"I can be," the creature said. "I'll move out of your way if you prefer. I know this is your path."

The creature politely moved to one side and gestured for them to pass. Jarl went past him without hesitation and after a long moment, Keisha followed, glancing at the creature warily as she walked past him. Once they were past, the creature joined them on the path and Keisha stopped again, looking bewildered.

"Are you going to follow us?"

"Unless you object," the creature said. "I'm curious about you. Aren't you curious about me?"

That was the same technique Arlen had used, he realized. They were trying to approach humans the same way Arlen had, probably hoping that humans would react the way he had. He was relieved, but also a little irritated that they thought all humans would act the same and respond to the same stimulus. Still, Keisha did look curious. Maybe it was a good strategy.

They walked in silence, Jarl and Keisha next to each other in the path and the creature immediately behind them as the path only allowed two people to walk next to each other comfortably. Jarl looked back at him, wondering if Arlen planned on joining them at any point.

"I think one creature is enough," he said. "I hope we don't see any others."

The creature looked surprised, but nodded. "I'll make sure we don't."

Jarl felt a low pulse in his mind, a command to stay away. He didn't know if it was directed at Arlen specifically or at all of the creatures but he was reassured. Keisha could handle one creature, but not more. And he didn't want to have to hide his feelings for Arlen.

They walked another hour and then he could tell Keisha needed to rest. He found a small hollow where they both could fit and she looked at the creature.

"Aren't you leaving?" she asked nervously.

"Would you feel safer?"

"Yes," she said without hesitation.

The creature grinned and she shivered. The fangs were not reassuring and Jarl had forgotten how large they were. "Then I'll leave."

The creature headed into the woods and Keisha looked at

him.

"You really saw one of those? It helped you?"

"Yes," he said. "They can't hurt us right now, remember?"

"Was that why you were lured into the woods when you returned?"

Jarl was silent for a moment, not knowing how to answer.

"Yes," he said, deciding to go with the truth. "That one will lure you out as well. But you'll survive."

"All I have to do is look at the moon, right?" she asked, not nearly as frightened at the thought of being lured as Jarl had been. He smiled and nodded, but inwardly he wondered if that would be enough to satisfy the creatures. They wanted people to adapt, like him, not simply survive.

He woke when it was still dark and could sense the creature nearby, though he couldn't see him. Four days left. He shook Keisha awake. She needed to learn to wake earlier on her own, he thought. He would point that out to Doss. They needed to reach the plants tonight or they would be behind and might not make it back on time. She was groggy but got up obediently and they got ready for the day quickly. Soon they were on the path again and the creature appeared as if out of nowhere, though Jarl had felt him coming. Keisha flinched but the creature smiled in what Jarl knew was meant to be a reassuring way. Keisha did not look reassured.

"Did you sleep well?" the creature asked her.

"No one sleeps well in this place," she said shortly, and Jarl realized he hadn't had a single nightmare this past year. He hadn't mentioned it to anyone, but he hadn't realized just how long it had been since the kinds of dreams that were a trademark of living on this planet.

Jarl focused on making good time and the creature kept coaxing Keisha into talking to him, and she was beginning to loosen up. It helped that Jarl was here and wasn't threatened by the creature, he knew. She felt safe because he felt safe. They didn't talk much in the morning but when the creature returned as they approached the plants, she began to open up. She was far more willing to talk to the creature than he had been, and soon her curiosity was leading to ask all sorts of questions, far beyond the basic topics he and Arlen had talked about. He was almost jealous at how quickly their relationship was forming. Arlen had his heart, but they had never had this kind of casual conversation before.

"We're here," he finally said as the phosphorescent plants came into view. She let out a breath of awe at the sight of them. "We'll sleep and harvest them in the morning."

"There are so many of them," she said, sounding almost dismayed. "We have to harvest all of them?"

"Every single one," he confirmed. "You can't leave any unless they aren't ripe."

She looked at the creature, who left into the woods without a word. She and Jarl got ready to sleep and went to the edge of the plants so the light would impact them less. He closed his eyes and dreamed of Arlen, a dream of longing. When he opened his eyes, he almost expected to see the creature, but Arlen wasn't there. He sighed. Three more days.

CHAPTER 13

The plants were all ripe, luckily, and it was nice being able to split the bags between them as they headed back on the path. The sun was still high in the sky when Keisha asked for a break. He sighed and agreed. She took too many breaks, but they were making good time. Still, would she be able to do this on her own? Surely he hadn't needed this many breaks when he took over this route.

"That creature," she said slowly. "He's not what I expected. He's almost like a friend."

Jarl thought about how quickly he had fallen for Arlen once the siren's wail filled his mind, and how he had offered his body as well as his heart. He had stopped Arlen from killing his body by looking at the moon, but he suspected it was Arlen feeding on his heart that had bound him to the planet. Was there a way to get Keisha to offer her heart and not her body?

"He's like a brother, isn't he?" Jarl said, and she looked startled and blushed.

"A brother? That's not exactly what I was thinking, but I guess you're right."

"You should try to see him that way," Jarl urged, because clearly Keisha was attracted to him sexually and if that happened, she might die.

"A brother," she mused. "I guess I'll see when he comes back tonight. He will come back, won't he?"

"Yes," Jarl said.

"Good," she said, and he urged her to start moving again. This time, he gave her all the bags despite her protests.

"You need to get used to carrying everything," he said. "It's difficult and slows you down, and you're already going slow. You need to know what it'll be like if you do this alone."

"I don't know why I'm training like this," she muttered. "The path is yours. It's always been yours."

"It was someone else's before it was mine," he pointed out. "And I didn't have someone to help me the first time. You need to move faster so you can get back on time."

She groaned but obeyed, and soon they were slowly making their way down the path. He took half of the bags after a while. They did need to get back on time, after all. When the sun was fully down, the creature appeared and took most of their bags and they moved even faster. If Keisha got help from the creatures every night then she could probably do this on her own, he thought. Otherwise there was no way she could manage.

He had never realized how grueling the path was even though he was shocked every year at how underprepared he was for the physical trials, but he had always been able to do it. She wouldn't have been able to do it without his help, or without the creature's help, and that worried him. If something did happen to him, the colony needed a way to get this pollen and she was the one in charge of taking over after him. He would definitely have to talk to Doss about her training.

When they went to sleep, Jarl stayed awake and just waited until she was sound asleep. Then he got up. The creature was nearby and he went to where he could sense him waiting. He realized he could see in the darkness. In fact, he had been able to see well this entire trip. Maybe being connected to the planet let him peer into its shadows. The creature looked surprised when he approached.

"Where is Arlen?" he asked softly, not wanting to wake Keisha.

"I thought you didn't want to see him," the creature said, equally quiet.

"I don't want her to see him," Jarl said. "But I want to see him."

"He's not nearby, but I'll summon him," the creature said. "He'll be here by the time you wake up in the morning."

"No sooner?"

The creature shook his head. "We assumed you didn't want to see him."

Arlen must have been crushed by that, he thought. He remembered how upset he had been when he thought Arlen had given up on him after he was unable to get to the woods after being summoned the first time, and how hurt he had been as months passed in the colony and Arlen didn't come. He didn't want Arlen to experience that kind of rejection. He should have been clearer about why he didn't want to see Arlen, he thought angrily. He should have explained to this creature why it was dangerous having Arlen where Keisha could see him. Because he still didn't want Keisha to see him and if he couldn't get here until the morning, then he couldn't see him then.

"I don't want Keisha to see him," he said. "If he comes in the morning, there's no way to avoid that. But I need to see him. I'll wait until Keisha is asleep again tomorrow night. Can I see him then?"

"Yes," the creature said, then added, "He's hungry. You're his only food source now and he didn't feed from you properly last time. He's gotten weak."

Jarl winced, his heart aching at the thought of a weakened Arlen thinking Jarl had rejected him.

"He can feed tomorrow night, then," he said. "I didn't know he was weak or I would have asked him here earlier. Why didn't you tell me?"

"You're clearly hiding things from her," the creature pointed out. "I didn't know what was appropriate to tell you."

"Do you think she'll survive?"

"You barely survived," the creature pointed out. "If she offers me what you offered Arlen, I might kill her."

Jarl blushed and looked away, humiliated that this creature knew about what should have been something private between him and Arlen. He didn't like to think about the fact that other creatures had watched. He hadn't had control over his actions, after all, and had been desperate to offer himself. But even though it was instinct driving him to offer himself, he still felt ashamed that his impulse was to offer himself sexually in a public setting. If he had just given his heart, he would be able to stand the thought of what had happened, but because he had given his body, too, he was too embarrassed to look at the creature for a long moment.

"I don't think she will," he said. "I told her to think of you as a brother. You don't offer your body to a brother."

"Let's hope that works," he said. "I like her. I wouldn't want to kill her. But you should rest. Tomorrow is your long day and she seems to be slowing you down."

"She's not suited to this route," he agreed, wondering how the creatures knew his route so well. Did they always track him? He supposed it wouldn't be unusual and if these plants were designed with humans in mind, the creatures probably knew the routes and how long it took humans. "You'll make sure Arlen is here tomorrow night?"

The creature grinned, baring his fangs, but it invoked no fear, just a longing to see Arlen's smile.

"He'll be here," he promised. "Now sleep."

CHAPTER 14

Jarl's dreams were filled with excitement and the usual longing, and when he opened his eyes it was still dark. Two days left. He probably could have had time to see Arlen before Keisha got up, he considered, but they needed to start moving, not spend time talking. He shook her awake and she grumbled but got up. The creature appeared and helped them get going, and as the sun started to rise, he left and Jarl gave her all the bags again.

"I don't see how this is fair," she complained. "If I weren't here, you would be doing this all by yourself. Why are you dumping it all on me?"

"Because I can do this on my own," he said. "You can't, and you'll never learn unless you get real practice. Let's go."

After only two hours, though, he took back half of the bags. She just moved too slowly and they needed to get farther than she would be able. After a few more hours, he took all of them. Even though she wasn't getting tangled up in bags anymore, she was barely able to keep up. He tried not to snap at her as she asked for break after break but as afternoon stretched into evening, he couldn't help it. Not only was he starting to feel the pressure of getting far enough on this most important day of walking, he knew he needed to get to a good resting place as soon as possible so he would have more time with Arlen. He could not afford to be walking half the night.

When the creature showed up, he offered to take all of the bags and Jarl gratefully accepted the help, but it didn't matter much. After about thirty minutes, the creature gave the bags back to Jarl and instead helped Keisha, assisting her over the many branches and rocks that barely gave Jarl pause but seemed to slow her down tremendously.

When he and Arlen had been walking back, they had both easily been able to traverse the path. There had been no problems at all. In fact, he wasn't even aware of how many obstacles there were when he took this path, but now he was keenly aware of all of them. As he walked, he tried to stretch his awareness to feel Arlen and to his delight, he felt a hint of a pulse that he knew was him. Arlen was tracking them, near them, but not showing himself. Jarl tried to move them faster so he could reach Arlen sooner, but it just didn't help.

It was long past dark when he finally reached the point where he usually stopped on these trips. There were no specific markers as the landscape changed every year, but he had a good feel for it. He cursed Keisha for her slowness because it meant less time with Arlen. This night, she requested the creature stay with them and he was glad, because that made it slightly more likely that she would survive being drawn into the woods and it meant he could distract her if she woke up for some reason. As soon as she was asleep, he got up. The creature pointed into the woods in the direction he sensed Arlen and he nodded in thanks, then set out. He had only gone a short distance when Arlen appeared in the trees in front of him.

Arlen seemed different and he drew in a sharp breath. He was weak. His powerful form had grown thin, and he was breathing heavily. But his face was still beautiful, everything about him was still beautiful, and Jarl rushed forward to hug him. He took Arlen's hand and placed it over his heart, pouring out his love and his sorrow and request for forgiveness for requesting that he stay away without an explanation. He could feel Arlen feeding deeply.

Arlen held him like that for nearly half an hour before his body began to recover its shape and he finally spoke.

"I thought you sent me away," he said.

"I'm sorry," Jarl said, holding his creature close and pouring more love into their connection. "I should have explained. I just didn't want you near her."

"I didn't know love could hurt," Arlen said, and Jarl winced.

"It can," he said. "It's called heartbreak. Love hurts worse than anything when it's denied. I'm sorry. I didn't mean to do it to you. I didn't mean to weaken you."

"Am I weakening you?" Arlen asked softly. "You're still offering yourself to me. You're not driven to do it, and I don't want to force you."

"I love you," Jarl said. "My heart is always yours. The only way you'll weaken me is if you hate me or leave me. As I did to you," he added in a whisper, leaning against Arlen's muscled chest. Arlen kissed the top of his head and he regretted that they couldn't really kiss. His fangs didn't frighten him anymore, but he didn't like them for that one reason.

Arlen continued feeding on him another twenty minutes until sleep and exhaustion began to drag at his senses, but he wouldn't stop before his creature was finished. Finally, Arlen stopped feeding on him and stroked his cheek instead of his chest. Jarl had hoped to offer his body as well, though not in the uncontrollable way he had offered it last time. He wanted to have sex with Arlen properly, when that siren song wasn't driving him, but he was too tired now.

"You should rest," Arlen said gently. "You need to return tomorrow."

Jarl shivered. "I can't go back," he said.

"They need you. This girl can't handle the path on her own."

He sighed. It was true, unfortunately. But there had to be some way out of it.

"You're assuming she survives," Jarl pointed out. "Maybe they'll find someone else to train."

"Are you hoping she dies?" Arlen asked in surprise, and Jarl rushed to deny it.

"Of course not," he said. "But she isn't good for this path. We need someone with more endurance."

"They need you," Arlen said gently. "If you come alone next year, I'll be with you the entire time."

"That's true," he said, leaning against his creature.

He didn't have a scent, he realized. He had never noticed that before, but Arlen didn't smell of anything. He didn't want to go back to the humans with their smell, the humans that some made him queasy even though there was no reason for it. He didn't want to leave Arlen like this for another year. Would Arlen survive another year without feeding on him? He wasn't sure. He couldn't risk his creature coming to the colony again. They had gotten away with it once; that wouldn't happen again. Ender had never said anything and their relationship was stable now, without any of the fights that the others in the colony had worried about.

The president had even pulled him aside and asked if he was comfortable with Ender as a partner and he had reassured her that he was. He wasn't sure what would have happened if he hadn't, but he suspected Ender would have been kept away from him. And Ender would have talked. So he kept Ender close and he did enjoy their time together, but every time Ender entered him, he wished it was Arlen. He could not go back to that.

"I don't want to go," he whispered. "You can't make me go back two years in a row. You can't."

"They need you," Arlen repeated, though he sounded just as torn about this as Jarl felt. At least he didn't like the fact that Jarl had to return. Why did both of them need to keep sacrificing? Why did it matter so much that the other humans survive and adapt?

"They'll live without me," Jarl said. "And if they don't, they don't."

Arlen drew in a sharp breath. "You would abandon your fellow humans?"

"I've done everything in my power to help them adapt," he said. "I've helped Keisha get used to the creature here so she'll survive when she's drawn out here again. If she survives, if she adapts, why do you need me?"

Arlen was silent, and then he felt a pulse of music in his mind. A summons. He led Jarl a little farther into the woods and he felt exhaustion beginning to creep over him. Even if he stayed here, he had to get Keisha back tomorrow. She couldn't manage on her own. And for that, he needed sleep. But he didn't want to sleep if staying awake might get him what he truly wanted: staying with Arlen.

Only a couple of minutes passed before other creatures surrounded them and he shivered, clinging to Arlen. He had forgotten how frightening some of them were. Then a large figure approached slowly and he recognized the tree who must be in charge of all the creatures. He wondered if it was drawn from someone's dreams and nightmares. Whoever it was had a broad imagination if that were the case, and he couldn't tell if a dream or nightmare had inspired it.

"He wants to stay," Arlen said without preamble. "We can't make him go back a second time."

"The humans need him," the tree said in a deep voice. "We need him. He's the only thing helping them survive."

"Keisha might adapt the way I did," Jarl said. "And all I do to help them survive is look at the moon. I can do that out here just as easily."

There were murmurs from the creatures and he felt a buzz of notes in his mind, though he couldn't interpret it.

"You wanted to part from us when you first returned," the tree said. "You tried to sever the link between you and our planet. Perhaps you will feel the same this time and be content with the humans again."

It took a second to remember what had happened for him to want to end his connection with the planet, but not too long. His sorrow for Kandor and his lost friendship hit him again, as did rage that the very creatures around him were responsible for his death.

"You killed my friend," he hissed. "Of course I didn't want to be connected with you."

"We must feed," the tree said gently. "We feed on what you

humans offer us. You know that. We aren't able to spare their lives unless they stop offering to us, and they only do that when you intercede."

He was silent, because he knew that was true. Arlen would have killed him if the moon hadn't prevented it, and he knew Arlen didn't want to kill him. The creature with Keisha didn't want to kill her, but would do it if she offered herself in a way that hurt her. They weren't intentional killers but they did still kill, and the grief from Kandor's death that he had successfully buried over the past year was seeping back into his mind despite the knowledge that whoever killed him wouldn't have been able to stop themselves. And people weren't dying anymore, he knew. Oh, they sometimes died, but being lured to the woods was no longer a death sentence.

"I can help the humans survive from here," Jarl said slowly.

"You would have to live with us, and you fear us."

He shivered and looked around at them. He did not want to be around them any more than necessary, but he did want to be around Arlen. The creatures seemed to be everywhere in the woods, though. It was probably too much to expect that they all stay away from him, though it was what he wanted. Could he live with these nightmares who killed his friends?

"I don't care," he said firmly. "I don't want to go back. You have another who might survive this year. You don't need me anymore."

Another buzz of notes and he realized it was the creatures talking to each other and deliberately leaving him out. They didn't want him to know what they were saying as they consulted with each other and with the planet. Carefully, he tried to send his longing to stay with Arlen to them and the notes paused as the creatures looked at him. They had heard the message, then. The notes started up again and Arlen held him close. He shut his eyes for a moment as weakness struck him. He needed sleep.

"You are weak, human," the tree said suddenly. "Are you still hurt by Arlen feeding on you?"

"No, I'm just exhausted from walking all day, and the past four days," he said. "Arlen doesn't hurt me."

There was a slow pulse from the planet and he finally understood it. It was a pulse of compassion and acceptance, and agreement. He could stay. He didn't have to go back. But he would need to assist the other human first, because the colony wouldn't survive without the pollen. And he would have to do everything in his power to ensure that she adapted.

"Thank you," he whispered, tears filling his eyes. The creatures dispersed and Arlen brought him back to the camp. He tried to push him away as they drew near but Arlen ignored him and led him into the camp itself, helping him into the hollow where he would sleep. Arlen kissed his forehead, keeping his fangs to himself as he always did when he kissed Jarl now.

"Sleep, Jarl," he said softly. "When it's safe to leave this girl, come find me. I'll be waiting."

Jarl was too tired to reply and sank into a deep sleep with dreams of joy and satisfaction. When he woke up, he still felt exhausted but now he was filled with resolve. It was the last day of the peace, and his last day with humans.

CHAPTER 15

They were going to make it, but it would be close, Jarl thought grimly as he urged Keisha to greater speeds. He hadn't decided where to leave her yet. He had planned on leaving earlier in the day but as the afternoon stretched on and they still hadn't reached the safe area where other humans worked to cut down the trees, he knew he needed to stay with her and keep her going. He wondered how Kandor's replacement had been and if he had this many problems. Seeing Keisha's difficulty was making him reconsider his request to leave. He didn't want to be alone among the humans but the plants were important and it was unlikely Keisha could handle this on her own. Finally, they reached the edge of the zone where they would definitely reach safety in time. He came to a stop and she looked at him in surprise.

"You need a break? You never need breaks."

"You need to carry everything the rest of the way," he said, passing her all of the bags he had been carrying. She didn't look pleased, but she took them. "Tell Doss that you need to improve your endurance, speed, and ability to wake up on time."

She scowled. "You don't need to tell me how badly I did. Just tell him."

"I can't," Jarl said. "I'm not going back with you."

"What do you mean?" she asked, genuinely perplexed. He took a deep breath.

"I'm staying out here," he said.

"You're killing yourself?" she asked in shock. "You can't, Jarl. We need you. I can't do this on my own. You can't just kill yourself like this."

"I'm not killing myself," he said, though he didn't know how to explain it to her. If she survived being drawn into the woods then she would understand, but not until then. "I know how to survive out here now."

"But why are you staying here? Don't you know what lives in these woods?"

"I thought you weren't frightened of the creatures anymore," he said, and she shook her head.

"Not that creature," she said. "You're right. He's like an older brother and he's been helpful. But he's not the only creature. There are others."

"If you came out here, do you think your creature would protect you?"

She hesitated and looked into the woods for a moment. "When you're drawn out here, you're not in control, are you? He said he would draw me out here after I returned, but I guess if it's him, I don't really mind. But you don't have a creature to protect you. You'll go insane out here."

"I do have a creature," he said. "I told you. I met him last year. He'll protect me."

"But what will you do when the wind picks up? You can't look at the moon every second of every night, Jarl. And why would you want to? Why don't you want to come back to the colony? Do you not like it there?"

"It's complicated," he said with a sigh. "But I'll survive. And I can't go back."

"Well, what am I supposed to tell them? That you just decided to stay out here? They'll try to search for you and then a bunch of people will get caught in the night. You're too important."

"Tell them I tripped and broke my leg, and wanted you to return without me," he said.

"You want me to lie?"

"I'm not going back with you and I don't want them searching for me," he said, because he honestly hadn't thought anyone would search for him. Thinking about it now, though, of course they would search for him. He was the only one able to do the long path. That was clear now.

"Look, you can tell them what you want, but if you tell them I was injured, no one else gets hurt," he said. "You're bringing back the harvest and that's what they'll care about most. But tell Doss. You need more training before next year."

"You can't seriously expect me to do this path alone," she said. "I barely survived it with you and my creature helping me. Look, it's starting to get late. Let's just go back to the colony and talk about things there."

"I'm not going back," he said firmly. "I don't want anyone looking for me. I won't die."

She looked hesitant and he pointed to the sun lowering in the sky. "You'll have time to make it to the colony carrying all those bags if you leave right now. You can't wait or you won't make it. I'm not going with you, and you can't talk me into it."

"Jarl," she said, voice catching. She didn't seem to know what to say. "Thank you," she finally said in a soft voice. "If you're still alive when I'm drawn out here, I hope I see you."

"Maybe you will," he said, then gestured. She started heading down the path, looking back at him several times. He could sense Arlen nearby and as soon as he was sure she was going fast enough to make it in time, he headed into the woods in the direction he could tell Arlen was waiting. He walked for only a few minutes when a chill fell over him and he whirled. The female creature who had tried to feed on him when he was lured out here stood behind him and he edged backwards, hoping Arlen would risk coming close to the colony to help him.

"You belong to the woods now, human," she said in a cold voice. "You'd better get used to us."

She bared her fangs and hissed at him, then darted towards him. He stumbled backwards, falling to the ground and barely cushioning himself as he fell into a patch of spined ferns. He winced as they pierced his hands but he had caught himself in time. The creature hissed again but didn't attack. She just loomed over him for a moment as his heart trembled in his chest, then she turned and left.

He took a deep breath and stood up. What was she even doing out here, he wondered. They were close enough to the colony that she shouldn't have risked it during the day. Arlen was waiting farther in the woods where it was safe. Why had she come out here? Just to threaten him? It had worked, he admitted. He was terrified of her and many of the other creatures. He didn't especially want to live out here with them but he did not want to return to the colony and be locked away from Arlen.

He wiped his bloody palms on a nearby leaf, not wanting to get it on his pants. He realized with a start that he had nothing with him, only the outfit he was currently wearing. He had been wearing it for five days now and normally shedding his sweat and scent filled clothing and taking a bath was one of the joys of returning from the harvest. He wouldn't get that this year and shivered.

What was he going to do? And what was he going to eat? Were there other plants he could eat that the original colonists hadn't know about, or that were too far away for the humans to get to them? He should have thought of all of this before making this decision, he realized. Should he go back? He turned to the colony. If he went back right now, he could make it. If Keisha were smart and said he had been injured, then he could just say that he recovered and made it back on his own. He could still make it back.

But he would be trapped. He remembered the last year, feeling like an alien among his people, unable to participate in his life as fully as he once had because he was missing Arlen. He knew that Arlen fed on him, but he almost felt like he fed on Arlen, too. He needed him. The world only became real around him. In the colony it was like moving through a dream and he needed reality. But maybe he would prefer a dream. Now that he was no longer plagued by nightmares, he had realized that dreams could be pleasant. Reality was harsh and violent.

Wouldn't he rather be in the dream of the colony than out here with these creatures who killed without a thought and lured innocent humans to their deaths every night?

He took a step towards the colony. The sun was sinking rapidly. Keisha should have arrived by now, to at least gotten close enough that someone would have seen her and helped her get the final stretch. They would be watching for her, he knew. He took another step towards the colony. He might be able to make it. If he ran, he could certainly make it. But did he want it?

He shivered. No. He did not want the colony. He didn't want to go back to meaningless work and he didn't like to think of how the president had laughed off the claim that they were all equal. There was a clear hierarchy that he had never been aware of before but this past year it had become clear. He was vital to the survival of the colony but that also meant he had less freedom than most.

He had never noticed it before but all his work was fairly easy and didn't put any physical strain on him. It couldn't, because they needed him in perfect shape for the harvest each year. His relationship with Ender was similarly scrutinized. The president herself had involved herself in the relationship, though she didn't care about most couples unless they were petitioning to have a baby. They watched him carefully, and he had no freedom. He had never had any freedom, but he had never realized it before. Even Doss viewed him as a useful harvester and not really as a unique person.

It was the flaw of the colony, he realized. They were all supposed to work seamlessly together as a unified whole. Rather like the collective consciousness of the planet, he supposed. And he didn't want to be a part of it. He wanted to be his own person, unique and not subject to anyone else. In the colony he was owned by others; out here he chose who he belonged to. He wanted to offer himself to Arlen and he would, and he couldn't escape the music of the planet now but he could ignore it. He remembered how Arlen had once said he liked being an individual and Jarl agreed. He turned his back on the colony and made his way deeper into the woods, taking off his mask and letting it drop to the ground. Either the planet accepted him or it didn't. There was no point hiding anymore.

CHAPTER 16

Jarl hadn't gone far into the woods when he saw Arlen leaning against a tree, waiting for him. He climbed over the fallen branches between them and Arlen embraced him. They were in dense forest, the kind he had never dared go in before. There were almost no paths to walk on and the undergrowth reached to his knees amidst the boulders and fallen trees and branches. He was frightened, though trying not to show it. The sun was lowering rapidly and he had never been out in the woods in the night outside of the four nights of the peace. He knew he was part of the planet now but he was still scared. Arlen stroked his head.

"You're sure about this?"

"Yes," he whispered. "I thought about it. I'm sure."

"No one knows what will happen to you tonight," Arlen said softly. "It's never happened before."

He was suddenly aware of other creatures around them, watching them.

"Is there somewhere else we could go?" he asked. "Somewhere I can see the moon?"

Arlen nodded and began leading him. He had spent the past four days annoyed at Keisha's inability to get around the simple obstacles in their path and now he wondered if Arlen felt the same about him, because he was struggling in the dense woods. Soon they reached a clearing similar to the one where Arlen had first shown him the moon. It was just rising and the last of the sun's rays faded into night. He shivered.

There were still creatures around them, though they stayed in the trees and didn't come into the small clearing. He could see flashes of moonlight on their fangs and it chilled him to the core, reminding him of the female creature who had threatened him. Was he really comfortable out here like this? Not comfortable, he knew. He would never be comfortable. But was it better than in the colony?

A wind picked up and he flinched as the music of the planet surged suddenly. He turned to Arlen without thinking and offered himself, unable to help himself. Arlen put his hand on his heart and held him close as he felt an echo of the desperation that had driven him that night a year ago. There was no desperation this time, but he still needed it. After a few moments, he gasped and pulled back enough to look at the moon. Calm filled him and the urge to offer himself faded. The moon filled his awareness as it had almost every night since he had discovered it. A scream ripped through the night and he started in shock, his gaze broken as he looked around. It was a man's scream, and it sounded terrified.

Arlen grabbed his chin and forced his head to look at the moon again.

"Look at it," he said softly. "That's the best you can do for them right now. Make them stop offering themselves."

He took a deep breath and focused on the peace of the moon again, letting it fill him. There were no other screams. Time passed in a blur and soon he felt exhaustion wash over him. Arlen helped him lie down on the ground, still looking up at the moon, and lay next to him. He reached over to hold his creature's hand and sighed. It felt like it did during the peace. It didn't feel like anything was different. His eyes slipped shut.

He saw a spinning orb in front of him and when he tried to look around, the orb encompassed his entire vision. It wasn't the moon; it was Ylse. He recognized the blue and green and brown masses, though a heavy layer of clouds blurred the edges. He could feel the planet deep in his soul, singing to him. And he felt how perfect it was. Everything was in balance. There was a cycle to the song, a rhythm that the creatures and plants of the planet followed. Birth and death happened naturally as part of the song and he could feel the planet's enjoyment of this rhythm. Then he saw a small ship approach and land on the surface. The colonists. Immediately the song swung out of rhythm and he could see ripples across the surface as the human's poison spread. Soon there was a yellowish glow to the area where he knew the colony was and he could feel how discordant it was in relation to the rest of the planet.

He felt the planet's attempts to send the song into the colony and could sense the humans within driven insane. He felt the planet attempt to copy the song of the humans, creating hybrid creatures that were part of her and yet not, and realized those were the creatures of the night like Arlen. They weren't truly from this planet, he realized in shock. They were part human. That made sense, as they were spawned by human dreams, but it was an odd realization to think that the planet herself wasn't sure how to treat the creatures.

He could sense the moon's influence suddenly, an outside force working with the planet to draw out the poison from the humans. And then he saw a beam of light from the moon strike down to the surface. The image seemed to zoom into him and Arlen laying in the clearing staring at the moon. Not this time, not tonight, but their first night together when he had first really seen the moon.

He saw his body outlined in the same yellowish aura as the colony and it was lessened in the moonlight. He felt the planet's hope, but it wasn't enough. He felt the song rise again, spreading into the colony to draw out the humans, and saw himself leaving. He flushed, not wanting to see what came next, but the scene played on despite his wishes. He saw himself leap into a kiss with Arlen and felt the planet's surprise, and then he saw the yellowish aura around him start to be drawn into Arlen. He saw the poison drawn from his heart into his creature, neutralized and made safe.

When all the poison had been drawn from him, he saw the planet attempt to reach out to him and he heard the song as he'd been hearing it this past year. He had become part of the planet. He had given his heart to the planet and in doing so, had ceased to be poisonous. He felt the planet's hope, but also her impatience for other humans to do the same, and frustration that they weren't all embracing this new path. He felt the creatures, who were still so oddly independent from her, urging patience, and he saw their hope about this year and what might happen with this peace. He saw himself under the moon again, as he was tonight, and he saw Arlen lean over him.

"Jarl," Arlen said, shaking his shoulders. He jolted awake. They were in the exact positions he had seen just a moment ago and he was disoriented for a moment. The music had subsided and the moon had set. The horizon was glowing with the coming sun.

"What were you dreaming?" Arlen asked with a fang-bearing smile. "You looked peaceful. I've never seen a human peaceful while they sleep."

"How often do you watch humans sleep?" he responded, sitting up and looking around. There were still creatures around. Arlen laughed.

"We often watch you during the peace. I watched you many times before I approached you."

Jarl shivered, not liking to think about the creatures spying on the humans when they believed they were safe. But they were safe during the peace. It was the only time humans and creatures could interact without the humans being driven to offer themselves and the creatures driven to feed on them. It was the only rhythm the planet could create to try to integrate the humans into its melody. Offering and feeding, with only a few precious days of relief.

"I dreamt of the planet," he said softly. "Of how she came to be. Of what I've done to her."

"You've saved her," Arlen said.

"Not yet," he pointed out. "I'm just one human, one they

barely listened to."

He sighed and looked around. "Did anyone die? Did Keisha survive?"

"We did not try to lure Keisha and the other tonight," he said. "We could see several areas where there were many guards. But others came, and one died. He did not look at the moon."

Jarl shivered. So that scream he had heard had likely been someone's death. But the man would have died whether he was out here or not. Keisha was safe for another night, but...

"What do you mean, the other?"

"The one on the next longest path," Arlen said. "Jonah? One of us approached him. He seemed receptive."

"Anyone else?"

"We don't have time on any of the other paths," he said. "A few of us showed ourselves on the other paths but we didn't take time to talk to anyone. On most of the paths you humans can run back to the colony within a day if we frighten you, and we want to make sure you get to the plants and back."

That was true, he had to admit. So a creature had revealed itself to Kandor's replacement. If they lost both Keisha and Jonah, then the colony would be in a very bad situation indeed. Losing the harvesters from the two longest paths two years in a row would be deadly. He wished the creatures hadn't approached both of them, but he understood their impatience now. They wanted to neutralize the humans' poison and this was the only way they knew how.

"When will you lure them here?"

"When the guards leave. It may take a few days, as it did with you." Then he grinned. "You survived the night, Jarl. No human has ever done that. I was worried when you offered yourself to me at first."

"It wasn't the same," Jarl said with a blush. "I wasn't desperate last night. It was just... a craving. An instinct. The music wasn't nearly enough to make me lose my mind."

"I'll stay close to you every nightfall," Arlen promised. "I don't want you offering yourself to anyone else."

Jarl shuddered at the thought. What if he had instinctively offered himself to another creature? He had pulled back quickly to look at the moon, but if he had offered his body so a creature and it started to eat him, he might be crippled. He didn't want to be injured out here.

"What do you do during the day?" he asked. "Do you sleep? I'll have to change when I sleep."

Arlen laughed. "We have no need of sleep."

"Then why do you leave every day during the peace?"

"You carry guns," Arlen pointed out, and he realized he still had his gun. He would never use it on Arlen but he didn't want to get rid of it. If something else threatened him during the day, he needed to defend himself.

"Are there other animals out here during the day?"

"There are," Arlen said. "Some are dangerous. I will stay with you and protect you, but the planet wants you to survive. That may change in time, but you're safe for now."

"Am I safe from the other creatures?" he asked, thinking of the female creature.

"We hear the planet's music, but we aren't compelled to obey," Arlen said. "We're individuals. If someone is determined to hurt you, they can. But I will be with you, and they would never hurt me just to get to you."

That wasn't especially reassuring but he had known there would be danger out here. He had accepted it. And there was nothing he could do about it now. He looked in the direction of the colony. He was completely alone now. Even if he tried to go back, they would never accept him. They might let him into the colony, but they would conduct experiments on him and question him and break him. He would never be among humans again, and he wasn't sure how he felt about that. He didn't want to be in the colony, but he hadn't really understood that he wouldn't see any humans at all. The longest he had ever been without seeing a human was the five days of the peace, and he had always been ready to see friendly faces when he returned. He supposed he might be able to see more humans in the peace next year, but that was a long way off and he had to survive until then.

His stomach growled and he pulled out the small bag he had kept that held his food rations. They were almost completely gone, as they were only designed to last five days. Arlen watched him eat the tough bits of dried meat and drink the remnants of his water. He tossed the empty bag and canteen to the ground.

"I'll need food and water," he said cautiously.

"Keep these," Arlen said, picking up the bag and canteen. "I can bring you to another plant but you'll need to carry the pods, and we may be traveling to places where water isn't easy to find. The planet will provide everything, but not all at once. You must learn to pace your eating and drinking to harmonize with her."

"I'll try," Jarl said. "But humans need food pretty regularly, and water too."

"I've watched you, and been with you," Arlen said. "I know what humans require. You will survive."

He drew closer and traced a hand down Jarl's chest.

"I need to eat, too," he said suggestively. "I enjoyed feeding on you last year. I was disappointed we couldn't do it when I came to your colony."

Jarl's cheeks heated but he turned into Arlen's embrace and stroked his face, gazing into those ebony eyes. He leaned up and kissed him softly, lips only.

"I wish we could kiss," he said with a sigh. "But I'll give you my body any other way you want."

"Will it kill you?" Arlen asked seriously, and Jarl chuckled.

"Not if we're doing it right," he said. "It won't be like last time, but it'll still be good."

Arlen slid his hand around Jarl's waist and squeezed him tight. Jarl blinked in surprise.

"Right now?"

"What better time?" Arlen asked in a husky voice. "Or is it something you only do at night?"

"Well, you normally do it at night," Jarl said, pushing back slightly. "But I'm filthy. I've been wearing this for days and I need to bathe before I even consider something like that."

Arlen smiled and took his hand, leading him into the woods. He followed, wondering if this was going to be his life from now on, following and scrambling over boulders and branches and struggling to keep up. Arlen seemed to move through the woods effortlessly and he thought of how Keisha had struggled at even basic obstacles. This had to be how she felt. He hated it.

Soon they had made their way into the depths of the forest where the sun only barely filtered through the thick trees. It was terrifying, as the woods were closely aligned with death in his mind. Anyone who went in the woods died unless they kept to the specific paths they were taught and it was during the peace. He had only gone off the path once, with Arlen, to see the moon. He had never been this lost before and knew he could never get out on his own. It was a strange feeling of helplessness and he didn't like it.

He heard the sound of water nearby and soon they emerged onto the banks of a river. He stopped and stared. He had no idea there was a river so close, and it was a large river, too, and looked deep. Depending on how deep it was, he might be able to cross it, but the current looked fast in the middle. Towards the edges, though, it lapped against the shore quietly. He looked at Arlen.

"I liked the pond you showed me better," he said. "This looks like I might get washed away."

"We'll stay in the shallows," Arlen assured him.

"Are there creatures in the water?"

"None that will hurt you," he said, and Jarl eyed the water cautiously. Arlen let the drapes of cloth that covered him fall to the ground and Jarl drew in a sharp breath. He had never seen Arlen naked like this and he was perfection. He licked his lips. He hadn't been ready for sex before but seeing Arlen like this, he was. Arlen went into the water until it lapped around his ankles and looked back at him.

"Are you coming?"

CHAPTER 17

Without a word, Jarl unstrapped his belt and set it next to his bag. He began peeling off his clothes with relish, not wanting to be trapped in them any longer. He could easily wash them in the stream, he considered. He didn't have soap but it was better than nothing. And he didn't have time to worry about that because Arlen was waiting for him with a soft smile that made his hands hitch as they pulled off his pants. He nearly fell over in his haste to undress but soon he was naked and Arlen was admiring his body.

He blushed, feeling distinctly unclean. He ran a hand over his chin and the start of the beard that had grown over the past five days. He always hated having a beard but it was inevitable to some degree during the peace, but now he wondered what he was going to do about it. The creatures didn't have facial hair; maybe they would recommend something. But Arlen didn't seem like he objected to the beard, and that was all that mattered right now.

Jarl approached the water and dipped his toe in. It was icy cold. He hesitated. Was it too cold? Well, it wasn't too cold for Arlen, so he stepped in and shivered as the water went up to his ankles.

"This is freezing," he said to Arlen.

"What temperature would you prefer?" he asked, and Jarl laughed.

"Warmer than this."

He felt a pulse in the notes in his mind and his feet were no longer cold. He stared at the water in surprise. Was it changing temperature? It began to grow warm.

"Stop," he said. He didn't want to get burned. Another pulse passed through him and he hesitantly stepped further into the water. It was perfectly pleasant. "Did you really make the water change temperature?"

"No," Arlen said. "The planet adjusted your perception of it."

"What?" Jarl asked, staring down at himself. The planet had invaded his mind and body and changed him? He felt violated.

"You're part of our planet now," Arlen said. "She controls you to some degree. You're still free. If you wish, you can break free and return to feeling the water as you did before. I just thought you would appreciate this."

"I do," he said slowly. "I just… didn't expect a planet to be able to influence me so easily."

"Her music is powerful," Arlen said simply, then took his hand and led him until the water reached their waists. The current flowed against them but it was easy to stand without being swept away. Just a little further, though, he could tell that the pace picked up and he would have trouble remaining in place.

"This is as far as we should go," Arlen said.

Jarl nodded and sank down in the warm water so that it covered his shoulders, then dunked his head under and ran his hands through his hair. He proceeded to clean himself thoroughly and to his surprise, Arlen helped. He remembered that he had cleaned himself and Arlen this way in the pond last year and blushed that Arlen still remembered how to clean a human body. He didn't have soap but the water was good enough for now. He would have to come up with something to stay clean but he would worry about it later. Right now, he just wanted to enjoy the warm water and the feel of Arlen's hands against his body.

Arlen's hand slipped between his legs and he gasped, clutching Arlen tightly. Arlen stroked him gently, firmly, and Jarl melted against him, unable to fight. It felt so good and the water was just the right temperature and he could feel himself getting hard.

"This is good, right?" Arlen asked softly, and he moaned and pressed against his creature, wishing he could kiss him properly. Instead, he kissed his neck and licked the droplets of water that had splashed there. "In the river?" Arlen asked, his hand sliding back to Jarl's opening. He gasped, but the question brought some sense to him.

"No," he said. They were too close to the current and he had never done it standing up before, so he wasn't sure how it would work. They might fall into the river and get carried away, and even though the water was deliciously warm, he knew he wanted to be on the bank with solid ground under him.

He led Arlen back and was suddenly aware of other creatures nearby, watching him curiously. His arousal quieted and he hesitated before stepping out of the water.

"Is there any way they could stay away while we do this?" he asked uneasily. "I don't want them watching."

"They're curious how this works when you're not being forced into it," Arlen said.

"Well, they can get their own human," he muttered, and Arlen chuckled. He felt a pulse and then the creatures faded back into the woods. Arlen wrapped his arms around his waist and pulled him the rest of the way onto the shore. Jarl looked around for somewhere soft to lay. There didn't seem to be any good places but the ground should be soft enough, he supposed. There was soil that turned into gentle grass after a few feet, and it was nearly ten feet before the undergrowth led into tall trees. They had enough space. He took Arlen's hand and laid down, pulling the creature over him with a blush.

He slid his hand down Arlen's chest and paused at his belly button. Arlen smiled eagerly as he kept going and stroked Arlen's massive cock. It started to get hard in his hand and he shifted as heat swept through him. He wanted this. He and Ender had been having sex regularly but somehow it wasn't enough. He needed it with Arlen to satisfy him.

The soil was soft beneath him and he could feel the prickle

of grass against the back of his neck as he leaned up and kissed Arlen's shoulders and neck, clinging to him with one hand while stroking him below with the other. Arlen's hands were just as bold, one caressing his chest over his heart and the other reaching between his legs. He gasped as Arlen's hand made contact and whimpered, already on fire. He bent one leg to give Arlen access and the creature slid his hand back to his opening.

"Slowly this time," Jarl whispered. "With your finger first."

He felt delicious heat slide through him as he said that. He had never requested something during sex before. He had wanted things, but never been bold enough to say it because he always assumed his partner knew better. He always assumed his partner had more experience and would know what he wanted. This time, though, he knew Arlen knew nothing. He could tell Arlen anything and the creature would think it normal. His heart pounded heavily and his chest clenched at the possibilities.

They were still dripping from the river and it helped slick him up as Arlen carefully slid his finger inside him and Jarl moaned softly from the pleasure. He entered him slowly, clearly relishing the experience with a slight smile. His fangs were exposed but he was enjoying himself and Jarl could feel his increasing arousal against his side as Arlen lay beside him and fingered him. Then his finger brushed against something and Jarl jolted in shock. Arlen stopped instantly.

"Did I hurt you?" he asked, already pulling his finger out.

"No," Jarl said quickly, reaching down to grab his wrist and keep him in place. "That felt good. Incredibly good. Nothing has ever felt so good. It just surprised me."

Arlen's lips curled and his finger slid back in, and in seconds he had found that spot again. Every time he pressed against it, Jarl's chest grew heavy and his cock twitched, and soon he was desperate for more.

"I want you," he murmured, trying to offer himself so Arlen would have no choice but to take him. Instead, Arlen bared his fangs in a grin and slid two fingers into him.

He whimpered and spread his legs wider, eager for every sensation as his creature gently stretched him and kept sparking against that place deep within him that made him moan. His fingers were so much longer than a human's finger, he thought almost deliriously. This felt so incredibly good. He wanted nothing more than to lie here with Arlen feeling him and he let the pleasure wash over him. Then Arlen withdrew his fingers and he sighed in disappointment. But there was no need, because Arlen just grabbed his leg and pulled him into position to enter him fully.

He braced himself for the entry but Arlen had relaxed him so well that it was smooth and he grinned in relief and pleasure as his creature finally entered him and he felt complete in a way he hadn't before. As Arlen began thrusting against him, he clutched at his shoulders and tried to pull him tighter. Arlen's hands curled around him, keeping him in place as he thrust harder. Jarl let out a cry as Arlen's cock hit that spot inside him and he nearly came. He gasped and struggled to contain himself. They were just getting started; he couldn't come yet.

Pleasure blurred and Arlen's movements seem to sync with the rhythm of the planet inside his head and suddenly the planet's melody moved in time with the creature's movements and Jarl's cries were part of the music, his indrawn breaths the pauses, and everything pulsed with the force of their love. The music was reaching a crescendo and suddenly it was too much for Jarl, too much physical pleasure and the rhythm pounding through his head, and he felt his body explode. The music surged and he felt Arlen come inside him, then the music began to slow and fade into the back of his mind. He drew in a shuddering breath and opened his eyes to see Arlen's smile. Arlen kissed him and pulled out, then kissed him again. He felt limp and completely spent.

"Again?" Arlen asked with a saucy smile, and Jarl couldn't help but laugh.

"I wish," he said. "I need to recover first."

"This is different, then," Arlen said, and he blushed as he

remembered their only other time together when he had demanded time after time after time, desperate to offer his body to the creature.

"Only once," he said firmly. "But... you did enjoy it? It was enough?"

Arlen rolled onto the ground next to him and pulled him into an embrace, cradling his head under his strong chin.

"It was perfect," he said. "The planet moved with us. Did you feel it?"

"I heard it," Jarl said. "That didn't happen last time."

"No, it didn't," Arlen said. "You didn't belong to the planet then. Do you think every time will be like this?"

"I don't know," Jarl said, then backed up slightly to look at him. He smiled cautiously. "There are other ways to do it, you know."

"Other ways?"

"I could be on top," he suggested, wondering if Arlen would allow a suggestion like this. After all, Arlen didn't know what was normal or what was taboo and scandalous. None of his partners before had ever allowed him on top, even the one time he had been bold enough to ask, but maybe Arlen would.

"You wish to enter me?" Arlen said with a smile. "You can. I'm sure I would enjoy it just as much."

"No, that's not what I mean," Jarl said, though he was a little surprised. He would have to keep that in mind for the future. Maybe he would want to try that someday. But it wasn't what he had meant to imply. "You would still be inside me," he said cautiously. "It's just... I would be on top of you, moving on you."

"I will do anything with you," Arlen said. "But you'll have to show me what you mean. I'm not sure I understand."

"You'll... you'll try it?"

"Anything to please you," Arlen said, kissing his cheek. Jarl's heart leapt. He hadn't rejected it, and it seemed like the creature meant it. What other fantasies had he pushed aside because he was afraid to ask? He had so many desires and had buried so many of them because they didn't align with what he knew proper sex should be. Ender had been by-the-books, but one of his earlier boyfriends had been willing to experiment with him a little bit. That boyfriend had taken him from behind, a thrilling experience he longed to repeat with Arlen. There were so many things he could try with a willing partner and he shivered in anticipation. But not right now. Right now, he was spent.

They lay cradled together in the wet soil and sparse grass until the sun was high overhead, then Jarl sighed and went back into the river with Arlen to clean. He washed his clothes as well and stared at them. He didn't especially want to get back into them but they were all he had. Arlen went to the nearby tree and pulled cloth out the way he had a year ago, draping it around Jarl. Was it better to dress like this, or should he keep dressing like a human? His clothes offered far more protection than this draping cloth, but they wouldn't last long.

He wouldn't wear them, he decided. But he wrapped his belt with his gun around his waist and tied his bag and canteen to the his belt as well, and he stepped into the boots that offered vital protection against the forest floor. He wasn't fully dressed as a human, but he also wasn't fully dressed as a creature. He was between, which was an accurate assessment of his position here in these woods. But he did tuck his clothes in his empty bag in case he changed his mind later.

"So what else do you do during the day?" he asked Arlen, who laughed.

"I will do that every day with you, and every night," he said. "But we need to get to the nearby plant to get you food. The humans have never found it and it should be ripe."

"Only one plant or a patch?"

"One plant," he said. "Perhaps humans found it but since it was so limited, they've never come back. But one plant is all you need."

"I'll need to store the pods somewhere safe," he said. "Do you have a home or something? Where do you live?"

"We travel," Arlen said. "We have no colonies or homes the way you do."

"Would you consider having a home?" Jarl asked, thinking of how difficult it would be to constantly travel. Maybe the creatures had no problems with it but he would feel unattached and dissociated without somewhere to call home. "Is there a cave or something where we could stay most nights, where I could leave things and be safe?"

Arlen considered. "There are several caves around. Most are occupied by other animals but I could request that they give us space."

"I don't want to share with an animal," Jarl warned. He didn't know what kinds of animals Arlen meant but he didn't want to share space with a dangerous beast who might kill him the moment Arlen turned his back.

"Then I'll kill the animal," Arlen said. "We will make it our home and other animals will know not to go near."

"You would kill another creature of this planet?" he asked in shock.

"All animals die," Arlen pointed out. "It is the rhythm of this planet. All animals kill. Even us creatures who feed on humans kill others sometimes. It is the way of our world."

"And things will kill me, too?" he asked uneasily.

"You have the planet's blessing right now," he said. "But you will have to learn to survive out here. I'll teach you to protect yourself," he added with a smile. "I saw some of the tools you humans have in your colony when I visited you and many would work for defense."

He looked around and Jarl became aware of creatures nearby. At least they had stayed away while they had sex, he thought with relief. Then he remembered how their lovemaking had altered the very music of the planet and blushed. Maybe they hadn't been alone. Had everyone connected to the planet felt that, or just him and Arlen?

"Fill up your canteen," Arlen advised, gesturing to the river. "The path to the plant will take much of the day and we won't have access to water while we walk."

Jarl obeyed, taking off his boots and wading out just enough to get water from the depths that wouldn't have sand in it. He rubbed his feet dry on the grass before pulling the boots back on and looking around.

"Which way is it?"

"I'll have to teach you to sense such things," Arlen said, then pointed. "But for now I'll lead you. Let's go."

CHAPTER 18

The pollen pods were ripe when Arlen finally brought Jarl to the plant. He collected them in his bag and felt a flash of remorse that he would never be doing this for the colony again. He did look forward to being able to eat the pollen whenever he wanted, though. At the colony the pollen was reserved for certain members of the colony who needed its nutrients most, and everyone else subsisted primarily on other, less satisfying food. Another way the colony had discriminated against people without him even noticing, he thought.

The plant ought to have enough to last him the year if he were careful and Arlen had said there were two other plants they could go to over the next week to harvest to be safe. The plants were in season for three weeks and he needed to get enough to last him the rest of the year. The colony grew much of its food, but the plants they used weren't native and there was no way he could grow anything out here in the woods.

The sun was setting as Arlen brought him back towards the colony with his pods in tow. They arrived at a small clearing with a large rock in the center and Arlen gestured to it.

"For now, this can be our home," he said. "The other creatures will stay away from this clearing and other animals will, as well. For the night at least. You can leave your things here safely tonight."

"Thank you," Jarl said, setting down his bags and water canteen. He sat down and leaned against the stone, feeling worn out. He trained all year for the five days of the peace and usually when it was over, he rested and recovered. Today, though, had essentially been a sixth day of the same strenuous activity and he was exhausted. As the sun slipped beyond the horizon, he felt the wind rise and the music surged through him. He turned to Arlen, who was waiting for him, and offered his heart without thinking. Arlen placed a hand on his chest and Jarl took a deep breath and regained control. The music lessened in his mind. He needed to look at the moon, he thought, and started to look up.

Arlen laid his hand over Jarl's eyes and he started in surprise.

"What are you doing?" he asked as the wind rushed through the clearing. "I need to look at the moon or people will die."

"Not tonight," Arlen said, tightening his trip on Jarl. "You cannot interfere tonight."

Jarl tried to yank his hand away but Arlen pinned him to the rock, hand completely blocking out all light. In the distance, he heard a scream. He struggled harder.

"You have to let me go," he begged. "They're going to die. The humans are going to die."

"You cannot help them tonight," Arlen said. "You must let this happen."

"No," Jarl cried, elbowing him hard to try to loosen his grip.

Arlen slammed him to the ground unexpectedly, twisting his arm behind his back while keeping his eyes covered. He suddenly felt the presence of other creatures around him and tensed. Were they going to kill him? Had they just lured him out here to kill him? He remembered what the oldest woman had said about the planet saving him for a worse fate. What if she were right? What if they had allowed him to survive just to lessen the colonist's fears of the planet and now the planet was going to take all of the humans at once? What if Arlen had been lying to him all this time, just waiting to betray him?

He struggled against Arlen's arms and against the music in his mind and against the creatures he could sense nearby, trying to free himself so that he could protect the other humans. But no matter what he did, the music rose louder to drown out his efforts and he was completely helpless against them.

The music surged in his mind but for once, it wasn't urging him to offer himself. It was urging him to wait, to be patient, to let it wreak its murderous havoc on the innocent humans it must have lured into its grip. He fought, but there was nothing he could do. And then there was silence.

It happened so suddenly he wasn't sure what had happened, but all of a sudden, the resounding chorus in his mind dropped to a tinkling of bells in his subconscious. Arlen let him go and he opened his eyes slowly and looked around. There were five creatures surrounding him and Arlen tentatively touched his arm. The moon was shining and Jarl looked at it, though he knew it was likely too late for whoever else had been out this night.

There was a pulse along the notes in his mind: a summons. He couldn't disobey as Arlen led him closer to the colony. He shivered. Did the planet want to show him the humans they had killed? He had seen many bodies on collection duty in the colony but he had never had to see the bodies along with the creatures who had just fed. Would he ever be able to look at Arlen the same way if he saw other creatures with their victims? What did the planet want from him? Why had it prevented him from saving other humans but left him alive?

They reached a clearing and Jarl winced at the sight of a creature cradling a human form. It was Keisha and Jarl shivered. But then she stood up, wobbling slightly as her creature steadied her. The creature's hand was on her heart and as she looked around, her eyes caught Jarl's and he drew in a slow breath. She was unharmed.

"Jarl," she said, sounding stunned. Not nearly as stunned as he was.

"Keisha," he said, and took a step closer.

"What happened?" she asked, looking from him to the other creatures.

"You adapted," her creature said with a pleased smile. "You offered me your heart only, and survived."

Jarl couldn't hold back a laugh of relief. She hadn't offered her body, only her heart, and she had survived. There was a rustling and he felt other creatures arriving, and then a female creature came into the clearing with them holding a limp and bleeding human form. Jonah, the other forager. But even though he wasn't walking on his own and appeared badly injured, he was alive. His creature helped him to his feet and Jarl blushed as he realized the injuries were sexual in nature. Apparently Jonah had offered himself the same way Jarl had, and likely had the same types of injuries.

"Jarl?" he asked hoarsely, then looked at Keisha. "What's going on?"

"You survived the same way I did," Jarl said. He looked at the other creatures. "What happens now? Are you going to make them go back?"

"Go back?" Jonah asked in shock. "You can't make us go back. They'll kill us."

"You must go back," his creature said. "You must teach the others the way that Jarl taught you."

"But he didn't teach us anything," Jonah said, then paused and looked at Jarl. "I guess you did. If I hadn't looked at the moon, I think I would have kept… I wouldn't have survived."

"He taught me everything," Keisha said. "But how are we supposed to teach others? What are we supposed to tell them? That you're not enemies? We'd be killed."

"I don't know what else they can say," Jarl said, agreeing with her. "I told them to look at the moon and they do, now. I don't think anything we do can get them to accept creatures."

"Persuade them to come out during the next peace and talk to us," the creature said. "The more of you we talk to, the more will be safe."

"So we're safe?" Keisha asked, looking at her creature.

"The planet will not hurt you anymore," he said. "You belong to it now."

"Being immune to the planet does not mean she won't hurt you," hissed the female creature who had threatened Jarl. "You are now subject to the planet's wishes, and death is part of the rhythm of our planet."

Jarl shivered and Arlen glared. "The planet wants the humans to survive. Until all of them adapt to her will, she will protect them."

The female creature looked straight at Jarl and smiled cruelly, not saying a word. He shivered again. The planet might not be a threat to him, but she was. He wondered why she was so determined to hurt him. In his dream of the planet he had gotten the impression that the planet wanted the humans to adapt and survive, but she seemed to be trying to sabotage that process. Then again, he had also sensed that the creatures weren't as strongly connected to the planet as the other animals, so perhaps she was more independent than the others. He wondered how the other creatures felt. If the only way for humans to adapt was to spend time with creatures and learn to love them, then he wanted to be able to trust the creatures' intentions. What if a creature like her seduced a human and then devoured them? The humans would never trust the creatures if that happened.

Keisha and Jonah looked at each other uneasily, probably as unsure of the female creature as Jarl was. But he wanted this to work, so he smiled at them.

"We're safe here," he said. Then he looked at the elder creature. "But I really don't know if anything they say can persuade the others to talk to you during the peace."

"We must try," the creature said solemnly.

Jarl nodded. The creatures could only approach the humans on the two longest routes right now and it was likely Keisha and Jonah would continue on those routes, so there wouldn't be a chance to talk to different humans next year. The colony couldn't keep training new people for those routes. There just weren't enough people capable of it. Even Keisha could barely get through it and she had plenty of help.

"They've had a year to get used to the idea that the woods aren't a death sentence," Jarl said to Keisha and Jonah. "Tell them that you looked at the moon and the creatures talked to you instead of eating you. Then, throughout the year, talk to the younger people and tell them that the creatures want to befriend us during the peace. Tell them to sneak out during the peace."

Jarl looked at the creatures. "You might need to get closer to the colony if you want to talk to the people who sneak out. They can't go far."

"We can only go at night," the elder creature warned. "We will not risk ourselves to your guns."

Jarl nodded and looked back at the other humans. "Tell the younger people to leave at night, and to come back every night of the peace. Tell them to try to avoid being seen."

"You really think that'll work?" Keisha asked nervously.

"Don't let the president know, or the old timers," he warned. "They're dangerous. Tell them you talked to the creatures but that's it."

"What am I supposed to do?" Jonah asked, gesturing to his bloody and battered body. "Why would a creature talk to me after attacking me? They're going to assume it was an attack."

"Tell them you were attacked, then looked at the moon, then your creature talked to you," Jarl said. "And tell them to think of the creatures as brothers and sisters," Jarl added, thinking of how he had saved Keisha from the attack. Keisha blushed and looked at Jonah, probably able to figure out what had happened differently between them and how Jarl's comment to her had saved her from offering herself sexually. Would Jonah's injuries be a problem? A doctor could probably tell he had been injured during sex but maybe he would assume the sex occurred before the attack, as he had assumed in Jarl's case. He would have to hope. If the colony thought creatures were attracted to them, there would be even more fear than before.

"You're not a sister to me," Jonah said softly to his creature, stroking her arm. Jarl wondered if he loved her now, the same way Jarl's love for Arlen had sprung out of friendship when the song of the planet had filled his mind.

"Are you coming back with us, Jarl?" Keisha asked almost desperately. "You seem to know exactly what to do and wouldn't they listen to you? You can prove that it's possible to survive out here outside of the peace. Wouldn't they want to know that?"

"For now, just tell them to try to talk to the creatures, and tell them it's only safe during the peace," Jarl said. "They can't accept too much at once."

Keisha and Jonah were much younger than him, he realized suddenly. No wonder they were afraid of doing this alone. He was an adult, confident in himself, but they were practically teens who were no doubt insecure of themselves. He smiled.

"You can do it," he assured them. "I believe in you. And you have your creatures to support you as well."

"But we can't see them while we're in the colony, can we?" Jonah asked sadly.

"We could try to visit you," his creature offered.

"You shouldn't," Jarl said, and Arlen nodded.

"There are too many dangers, and not just the guards," Arlen said. "It would not be wise."

Keisha's creature ran his fingers through her hair. "We can lure you to the woods again, perhaps," he said. "If you survive a second time and say you spoke to us again, perhaps it will help to convince them that we aren't enemies."

Jarl considered that option. It sounded reasonable. Plus, he suspected the creatures wouldn't survive an entire year without feeding. Arlen had been so weak, and he had gotten to feed halfway through. He couldn't ask the creatures to stay away from Keisha and Jonah all year.

"We must get you closer to the humans," the elder creature said. "You are weak and need rest. Do you know what to do and say?"

"Yes," they both said, sounding frightened.

"We'll let you say goodbye in peace," Arlen said, glancing at the other creatures meaningfully.

He took Jarl's hand and started leading him away as the others dispersed. As Jarl left the clearing, he saw Keisha's creature leading her in the opposite direction and wondered what their relationship was. Not physical love, but she had been able to give him her heart and survive. Would it be as difficult to say goodbye for her as it had been for him to say goodbye to Arlen? He wondered how they would arrange for Keisha and Jonah to be found, and he wondered what the colony's reaction would be. Would their plan work? They would have no real way of knowing until they drew Keisha or Jonah into the woods again, or until the peace next year, whichever came first. He felt almost abandoned not knowing what was happening in the colony but he had chosen his life out here, away from the humans. He didn't regret it yet.

CHAPTER 19

All of the pods and the water canteen were safe when he and Arlen returned to the clearing with the rock and he was reassured. The female creature frightened him but it seemed the rest of the planet would leave him alone. He gratefully slipped into a peaceful sleep and when he awoke, Arlen was sitting next to him, leaning against the stone. He sat up and yawned.

"We should head to another plant today," Arlen said. "It'll take two days to get there, and we'll be very far from the colony. Can you do that?"

"I'll do my best to keep up," he said, though the thought of more days of walking was a little intimidating.

He had always thought that he kept himself in good shape but he was realizing that his endurance was fairly limited. He could push himself hard for five days, but everything after that was difficult. The woods didn't make it easier with the fallen tree trunks and boulders scattering the ground and the low visibility with the dense trees and undergrowth. But he would try, and he knew he would eventually get used to it, just as he had gotten used to his route. He hoped Keisha would be used to the route by the next peace. Maybe he could arrange to be nearby and help her out. Assuming he survived that long, he thought grimly. He was alone now, with only Arlen to protect him. There was danger all around him and he would have to be extra careful not to injure himself. There were no doctors out here.

"Once we have all the pods, we'll find a home for us," Arlen said as they headed out. He was carrying the bags, freeing Jarl up to climb over the obstacles in their path. "It'll have to be near the colony so that we can assist if anything happens."

"That's fine," Jarl said, huffing slightly as rough bark rubbed against his palms. He was going to develop calluses quickly, he suspected.

"There are more creatures near the colony," Arlen said, glancing back at him. "They cluster at the colony. If humans start adapting regularly, I'll take you deep in the woods where there aren't any other creatures. But until then, we must survive nearby."

Jarl nodded. He hadn't even thought that the creatures would be concentrated, but of course they would be around the colony. That was their food source, and also where they spawned. Most of the planet probably didn't have any creatures at all. He was reassured that eventually he could live without fear of the other creatures, but it might be years before that happened. There were no guarantees he would survive that long.

Although Arlen had predicted it would take two days to reach the plant, it actually took three. Jarl was simply too exhausted and had to rest more than usual. He was careful to look at the moon every night, though he wondered if it was necessary with Keisha and Jonah doing the same. Although he hadn't told them to look at the moon every night, he realized with a start. They didn't know why people were surviving and there was no way to get a message to them now. It would be up to him to protect people by looking at the moon, at least until the creatures made contact with Keisha or Jonah again. He knew Arlen would be keeping him near the colony, but would he actually get a chance to talk to them? He wasn't sure.

Maybe he could try to tell their creatures to let them know to look at the moon, he considered. He tentatively reached out to the music in his mind and tried to sense any creatures linked to humans. He felt three notes stand out and tried to send the message to them through music, doing his best to limit it. Arlen stopped and looked back at him.

"You sent a message," he said in surprise, and Jarl blushed.

"How many creatures heard it?"

"Just the ones you sent it to," Arlen said. "I'm glad you thought of that. With them looking at the moon, perhaps you would be able to get more sleep."

That meant the message had been delivered safely and he was relieved. This could be quite useful, he considered as he continued to gaze at the moon. He wasn't very good at manipulating the planet's song yet, but he could learn.

In the morning he harvested the plant and they set out to the next one, only a day away. Perhaps two, Arlen had added thoughtfully, but assured him it would still be ripe. They set out and it was indeed two days, though Arlen didn't show any of the impatience Jarl had shown Keisha during their trek. Perhaps it was because they weren't rushing to accomplish everything before a deadline, but it was probably also because Arlen was simply a more patient person. Jarl was grateful for his silent support and soon he had enough pods to last a year, if not longer. Good. He wanted a stockpile just in case.

Once they had everything, they set out for a cave closer to the colony that Arlen assured him would be empty by the time they arrived. Instead of killing the animal who normally lived there, he had simply persuaded the animal to go somewhere else. Since the planet was on Jarl's side, the animal had obeyed without question. And sure enough, as another night was falling, they reached a large hill with a deep hole cut into it. The hole was barely tall enough to walk through but once inside it opened up considerably. The dirt floor was beaten down in the places where the animal or animals must have slept and it stank a little, but not nearly as much as Jarl was beginning to smell. He really needed to figure out a soap replacement. He had been bathing as often as possible but it didn't help much. Arlen hadn't commented, but he had to notice.

Jarl arranged the bags of pods into a corner of the cave. It was a single room with a few cubbies along the side. One could serve as a bathroom, he considered, so he wouldn't have to go outside every time. He would need a pot or container of some sort so he wouldn't just be going on the ground inside, but maybe Arlen could help him come up with something. He set his clothes in another cubby and then returned to the center, where Arlen was looking around.

"Does this work?" Arlen asked. "I know it's nothing like the colony."

"This should be enough," Jarl said, then looked at the ground. He had been sleeping on the ground for too long and ached for something soft to sleep on, and a blanket to cover him. "Could we get more fabric for a blanket?" he asked shyly. "And would anything work for a pillow or mattress?"

"There are several soft plants nearby," Arlen said. "Their petals would cushion you and serve as blankets, too. I'll go get them. You rest here."

"I can't see the moon," Jarl realized suddenly.

"Come outside," Arlen said. "You usually only need to look at the moon for an hour or two, and then you can come in and sleep. Your bed will be ready by then."

Jarl nodded and returned outside. Luckily there was a clear view of the sky and the moon was just rising. He stared at it and felt the usual peace sweep over him. He was so intensely grateful to the beautiful orb. It was the only reason he was alive, the only reason any of the humans were alive.

Without the moon, there wouldn't be a peace every year and the colony would starve. And now, the moon also protected the people who looked at it when they were drawn out. He wondered how many were surviving, and if he was looking at the moon long enough. The longer he looked at it, the safer everyone was, but he was running out of energy and couldn't stay awake as long as he could when living in the colony. He hoped people were still surviving unharmed, because that would make Keisha and Jonah's job easier. People needed to stop thinking of the woods as dangerous or else they wouldn't risk coming out during the next peace. Maybe he would stay out here a little longer tonight.

Arlen returned with an armful of pale blue petals that were thick and looked incredibly comfortable. Jarl touched one and it was like velvet. This would be perfect. He continued to look at the moon while Arlen went inside to arrange a bed for him. After a while, Arlen came to sit next to him.

"You're surviving," Arlen said. "And now you won't have to walk as far every day. We have food, the river is only ten minutes away for water, and we have shelter. What else do you need?"

"I'll need something to do every day," Jarl said. "I don't want to get bored. But for a few days I might need to rest. I'm not used to walking in the woods like this, not for this long."

"We'll take as long as you need, and then I can teach you how to live here."

Jarl smiled at him and was rewarded with a flash of fangs as Arlen smiled in return. He cuddled against his creature and gazed at the moon for as long as he could before his eyes began drifting shut. He wanted to stay awake, to keep his eyes open, but a hazy warmth spread through him and it felt like magnets were drawing his eyelids together. Arlen helped him up and they went inside. Jarl curled up on the petals and it was just as comfortable as he had hoped. He hadn't felt this comfortable in nearly two weeks and as Arlen pulled another petal to cover him, he gratefully sank into sleep.

CHAPTER 20

The rhythm of the planet pulsed through him as Jarl released the arrow and the animal cried out and fell to the ground, dead. He was getting good at hunting, he thought proudly as Arlen retrieved the rabbit. Four months had passed since he had left the human colony and he had learned to manipulate the planet to some degree, enough to persuade the planet to let him kill the animals here. If his arrows matched the swell of the planet's music, then he would strike true. Otherwise, the animal would survive even if he hit it. Everything on the planet moved with the rhythm, even life and death, and he had learned to read the music and start to persuade it to adapt to his individual needs.

"Good job," Arlen said. He was in charge of the animals after they were shot. Jarl was too squeamish to skin and gut the animals, and even felt a little nauseous watching them cook. But he was able to eat them without problems and Arlen didn't mind taking care of the rest.

Much of his diet was now supplemented by meat and the berries that grew nearby. He was tempted to start a garden, but didn't have any seeds. He felt safe in their home and while he could usually sense other creatures nearby, none had shown themselves.

Jarl had built a bow and arrow to hunt, not wanting to waste his bullets. The female creature still worried him and he wanted a gun in case he had to deal with her. He was safe for now, but kept his gun on him at all times just in case.

They returned to their home and Jarl went inside and sank into the petals as Arlen took care of the rabbit outside. It was late and he would have to go look at the moon soon. He couldn't forget. Luckily he had Arlen to remind him. Now that he wasn't faced with the results of each night's victims at the colony, it was easy to forget how absolutely necessary it was to look at the moon each night.

He had almost forgotten a couple of times but Arlen always remembered and he was always flush with shame those night he didn't think of it himself. He was the reason people were surviving and if they didn't keep surviving, then all of their plans for the future would collapse. He just had to hope that Keisha and Jonah were doing well in the colony and they were persuading the young people. They were young themselves so hopefully the message would be persuasive.

He wondered what the oldest woman had thought about Jarl's disappearance. If she somehow twisted it into something evil, some sign that the planet had laid a trap for him, then it was unlikely Keisha and Jonah could succeed. But if Keisha did as he recommended and said he were injured, and if the others believed it, then it should be safe. He should have asked Keisha what she said when she was here. He had thought of quite a few things he should have said or asked but there was nothing he could do now. Sometimes he missed humans deeply, even to the point of tears, but it was getting less frequent. Sometimes the thought of Ender overwhelmed him. He hadn't loved Ender, not really, but they had grown so close. He missed having humans nearby.

As night fell, Jarl went outside and laid on his back near their fire pit where Arlen was preparing the rabbit. Neither of them said anything; this was their usual routine by now. The moon was gorgeous, as always. At least he enjoyed looking at the moon every night. If he had to do something he hated every night, he probably wouldn't do it. But he loved looking at the moon and feeling peace and calm wash over him. He felt safe and protected under her light.

Three hours passed and he was just beginning to doze off. Arlen had come over to lay beside him and he sometimes fell asleep out here, leaving Arlen to carry him inside. He wasn't sure what Arlen did at night. He knew Arlen left most nights, but he was safe even without Arlen at his side. The moon and the planet protected him. As his eyes started to drift shut and he began blinking more often in the first signs of exhaustion, he felt the music swell slightly in a summons. He sat up, shaking the sleep from his mind as he and Arlen stood up.

"You felt that?" Arlen asked, and he nodded. "Did you sense what it was for?"

"Just a summons," Jarl said.

"It was from Jonah's creature," he said. "She must have lured him to the woods. Let's go."

Excitement wiped away any remaining sleep as they began the hike to the colony. He still had trouble telling where the music was coming from and was just glad he had Arlen to translate. Had Jonah come to the woods? What news would he bring? Anticipation coursed through him the entire hour it took to reach the woods outside the colony where the summons came from. He could sense other creatures converging as well, including the one he recognized as the tree-like elder. Then they reached the clearing where the elder stood with Jonah and his creature. Jonah looked happy. That was a good sign. At the sight of Jarl, Jonah's face broke into a smile.

"Jarl," he said. "You're still alive."

"So are you," Jarl said, embracing him and luxuriating in the feel of another human.

He was glad Arlen had shown him a mineral that erased his scent or else Jonah probably would have commented. He had been living in the woods for months without deodorant, after all, and if he hadn't cautiously asked Arlen about it, he would reek. Arlen had also taught him to manipulate the music within his own body to expel the hair follicles on his face, so shaving wasn't a problem either and Jonah actually stroked his smooth cheek as if wondering how he didn't have a beard. His hair was a different story; he had several blades, some of them quite sharp, but his hair was uneven and he knew he looked a little ragged.

"What happened?" Jarl asked. "How is the colony? Are people listening?"

"Yes," Jonah said, sounding proud. "I was just telling the elder. I think surviving tonight will help. A lot of the young people are curious, just like you said they would be. The old timers are suspicious. They don't like that you didn't come back."

Jarl winced. When he had decided to stay, it hadn't even occurred to him that the oldest woman might misinterpret it.

"But it's going well," Jonah added quickly. "We've learned how to avoid their notice. No one has died in the woods at all since the peace. Thank you for looking at the moon. Keisha and I can help now, too."

"Thank you," Jarl said, pleased that his efforts every night had been rewarded and even more grateful that he had Arlen to remind him on those nights when he forgot. "I'll still look at it as often as possible but it's hard out here."

"We'll take care of it," he said confidently. "People aren't afraid anymore. Sometimes people are injured, but not usually. And a few people even try to talk to the creatures when they're lured out."

"Really?" Jarl asked. No one had mentioned that to him, nor had he picked it up in the music of the planet. He glanced at Arlen, who looked equally surprised. At least he hadn't hidden it.

The elder smiled a fang-bearing smile. "We are not always able to respond," she said. "It is not true conversation. But it is a good start."

"I think it'll work this peace," Jonah said. "And if I can keep coming out here, then I won't mind being trapped there as much."

"How is Keisha?"

"She'll be jealous," he said with a laugh. "But you should wait a few more weeks before luring her. Otherwise it might be too suspicious."

The creatures nodded and Jarl wondered who had decided which of them to lure first. Maybe Jonah's creature grew hungrier because she fed on his heart and body. Or maybe it was just random. No, he thought, looking at Jonah's creature. He saw Keisha's creature at the edge of the group looking jealous. There must have been discussion and she had won the debate. Yes, he had definitely lost, and she had won. He wondered how arguments were decided among creatures. He might need that knowledge someday and he made a note to ask Arlen about it. He didn't see the female creature who frightened him anywhere and was grateful.

Jonah told them a little more about how things were going and Jarl asked about Ender. He was silent for a moment, which worried Jarl.

"He didn't react well to your, well, what they assume is your death," Jonah said slowly. "He tried to hurt himself. He was stopped, don't worry, but he's still really upset."

Jarl drew in a sharp breath. He hadn't expected Ender to react like that. He had known Ender would be upset, but they had never been in love. Or at least he hadn't been in love. Looking back, he realized that Ender had been in love with him. Deeply. He had lied about Arlen, after all. He had kept Jarl's secret even when sharing it would have been much easier. And ever since then, Jarl had been closer to him, more intimate with him, because he felt he owed it to the man. He hadn't even realized what Ender must have assumed about their relationship.

"You can't tell him I'm alive," Jarl said, his mind whirling. "But… I suppose you can't tell him anything. Will you keep an eye on him, for me?"

"I rarely see him," Jonah warned. "Keisha was the one who found out what he tried to do. She works with him sometimes."

"Then ask her. I don't want him hurt."

Jonah nodded.

"Everyone was upset, not just him," Jonah added. "Especially since Keisha told them she couldn't have handled it without your help."

"Does Doss think she'll be ready for the next peace? I can come help her, maybe, and she'll have her creature, too."

"We're training already," he said. "And a lot of younger people are training, too. They might send two people again on her route and mine, just to be safe. I wish they wouldn't," he added, looking at his creature. "I wouldn't get to see you then."

She stroked his cheek. "I can still see you at night while the other human sleeps."

Jonah nodded, and looked at Jarl. "Is that what you did?"

"Basically," he said, blushing slightly. He didn't want to admit that he had sent Arlen away until the very last night. He didn't like to think about his unintentional cruelty.

He went through all of the other questions and advice he had thought of in the past four months and soon felt like he knew everything he needed. Being away from humans made him miss the colony immensely and while Jonah didn't know most of the people he asked about, he could report on the general atmosphere of the colony, which was, for the first time, optimistic. Jarl's apparent death had been a blow, but even though the oldest woman had tried to blame it on the planet, no one had listened to her. Accidents happened, after all, and they were just grateful Keisha had been there to bring the harvest home. It sounded like things were doing well and before long, he felt a tug from Jonah's creature. She wanted to spend more time with him, so he stopped asking questions and thanked Jonah sincerely.

"Good luck," he added, and Jonah smiled.

"You too."

He and Arlen trekked back to their home and he laid down. Arlen curled up next to them. They often slept this way, or at least they fell asleep this way. Jarl often woke at night to find himself alone, but Arlen was usually at his side when he fell asleep and woke up. He couldn't expect his creature to stay with him when he didn't need sleep.

"You're sad," Arlen said, wrapping his arms around him. Jarl snuggled into him.

"Yeah," he said. "I'm happy too, though. Things are working well."

"But your friend hurt himself," Arlen said softly. "I'm sorry."

Jarl sniffled, unexpected tears filling his eyes. He hadn't thought he was as deeply connected to Ender as he was, but the thought of him in pain and hurting himself was unbearable. He hadn't let himself really feel the impact of that around the others but here, with only Arlen, he let sorrow overwhelm him. He had misled Ender, lied to him about the depth of their relationship. This was his fault. And he couldn't bear the thought of him in pain. Perhaps he did love him, he considered. Surely he wouldn't feel like this if there wasn't some level of love between them. And they had been lovers for nearly a year. How could feelings like that not spring up between them?

Arlen stroked his head as he clutched him and let his tears fall. Arlen said nothing, just held him, and it was everything Jarl needed. They stayed that way a long time as Jarl let out quiet sobs. It wasn't just Ender. It was the thought that he had really, truly left his world behind. It hadn't really struck him. He was alone out here in the woods, without any humans, but he hadn't fully realized that the humans would be living their own lives in the colony, without him. He didn't matter anymore, except possibly to Ender. The colony would move on.

Mourning wasn't encouraged and now that he was gone, he knew the president and even Doss would forget him quickly. They would be focused on the present and the future, not the past. He would be forgotten and he hadn't realized it would hurt this much.

He cried for hours until he finally fell asleep. In his dreams, he felt the planet embrace him and cushion him against his sorrow. He had lost the humans, but he had gained the planet, the moon, everything on this world. Was it a fair price to pay?

He thought of Arlen and felt content. He missed his colony and his people, but he was ready to live here with Arlen. He didn't regret his decision, no matter what had happened in his absence. He was ready to keep living, too. Maybe someday, when humans were adapting regularly and creatures weren't feared, maybe then he could return to the colony.

Would they even know who he was? Would they realize he was the reason they were surviving now? Probably not. He would just have to live with the knowledge that he would never really matter to them anymore and be content with the private knowledge of what he had done. He couldn't expect anything else.

CHAPTER 21

Keisha was drawn out to the woods two months after Jonah, and Jonah was lured a second time a few months later. Time passed in a blur as Jarl learned to more fully adapt to the planet. He felt confident living here now. He hadn't seen the female creature a single time but still carried his gun, wary of the dangers that the planet didn't control. And soon it was time for the peace and he and Arlen returned to the edge of the woods closest to the colony to see what happened.

All of the creatures were gathered and many were far closer than they had ever dared before. They would stay back during the day but most planned on getting quite close during the night when they were safer. He just hoped everything worked and enough people snuck out. And he hoped those people found good creatures to talk to, creatures who would earn their love.

As Jonah had predicted, he and Keisha were accompanied by other young people. He hoped all of them were ready for the long routes but there wasn't much he could do if they weren't. If it were just Keisha he could help her, but not with someone else there. He would have to explain who he was and how he was alive and that would be too much.

He and Arlen trailed Keisha and the boy with her until around noon and he was deeply reassured. Keisha was making good time and so was the boy. Assuming they kept that pace, they would have no problems. Doss had done a good job. And he could make out their conversation, which also reassured him.

The boy was asking about whether or not they would really see creatures, and whether Keisha had really spoken to a creature last time. That meant that he was ready to meet his own creature and also that Keisha's creature could openly spend time with her. A very good sign. He and Arlen returned to the edge of the woods and waited for night.

As the sunlight faded from the sky and the moon began her elegant ascent, the door to the colony creaked open and eight furtive shadows slipped out. Jarl grinned. The young people were sneaking out. He would have liked more, but eight was enough. They went to the woods in a bunch and seemed frightened, and didn't go in far. He felt pulsing music between the creatures as they tried to figure out what to do. Then one of the creatures decided to act.

He strode out to the edge of the woods, remaining safely in the trees but visible to the young people.

"Welcome," he said, angling his hands upwards the same way Arlen and Keisha's creature had. How did they know that was a way to indicate peace? They seemed to know quite a lot about human culture but there were some ways in which they were totally ignorant. It was hard to predict what they would and wouldn't know.

The people inched closer, looking at each other and whispering, probably having the same sort of discussion the creatures had just had: trying to figure out what to do. Just like with the creatures, one of the humans stepped forward.

"Are you a threat?" she asked warily.

"It's the peace," the creature said. "You're completely safe for the next four nights. Come, talk to us."

"How many of you are there?" she asked, still wary.

"Eight of us," the creature said, though there were far more than eight in the woods. Still, Jarl knew only eight would approach the humans. He wondered if they were the eight who were spawned from these people's dreams. There had to be creatures whose humans had been killed, and continued to feed on other humans. And there had to be creatures who had died, since there weren't nearly enough creatures to account for over a century of colonists. But he suspected that the eight creatures intended for these humans were close enough that they could approach. It seemed like every creature was nearby. Indeed, he felt a pulse and could tell that certain creatures were being called forward, but not all of them. Just eight of them, and he was certain it was the proper eight intended for these humans.

As the summons quieted, Jarl felt something cold nearby, at the edge of his awareness. He turned towards it. Whatever it was, it was a threat and it was coming closer. He looked at Arlen, who didn't seem to sense anything wrong. Was he overreacting?

"Arlen," he whispered. "Do you feel that?"

"Feel what?"

"Something dangerous, coming near," he said. Arlen stiffened and looked at him.

"You're sure?"

Jarl nodded. Arlen's eyes narrowed.

"It must be a threat to humans only or I would have felt it. Take me to it."

Jarl shivered but started leading him away from the humans. He fingered his gun nervously. What would be a threat to humans during the peace? Nothing on this planet could hurt them right now. He could feel it in the swell of the moonlight. Humans were completely safe during the peace. They drew closer and then he caught a glimpse of a creature moving towards them and froze. It was the female creature and she was the cause of the danger. Without thinking, he stepped into the path in front of her. She paused and Arlen was quickly at his side.

"Get out of my way," she hissed. "I have a right to one of the humans."

Was that true? It couldn't be. He could sense that eight creatures were already talking to the humans. They were all in a group but he could tell that each of the creatures had attached themselves to their human and were trying to persuade the humans to split up. It might be another night or two before the humans felt safe enough to do that and if he were closer he might have urged patience, but now he was faced with this threat and he wasn't sure what to do.

"The humans are intended for others," Arlen said calmly. "You have no place here. You were banished."

Jarl started at that. Why had she been banished? Because she posed a threat to him? He had wondered sometimes why he hadn't ever seen her since that first incident when he came to live in the woods. He hadn't expected something like this.

"We haven't been able to feed properly since this human came along," she said, gesturing to Jarl angrily. "He has destroyed the balance of our planet. She may not recognize the disruption but I do. He's destroying our world."

"He's saving it," Arlen said. "And balance is being restored. You should trust our planet when she says this is good. How can you defy her so openly?"

"She's being misled by these humans," the creature said. "Instead of neutralizing them, they've infected her. Their poison is misleading her. They must be destroyed."

Jarl shivered. He knew the creatures weren't feeding the same way since he was somehow making humans not offer themselves. He hadn't expected any creatures to be angry about that. Did they starve now? After all, they barely had anything to feed on. Were they dying off because he had stopped their food supply? Was he disrupting their entire world? The planet approved of him, he knew, but had he done something to manipulate her into that approval?

"You have no business with the humans," Arlen said firmly. "The planet agrees. All of us agree. We want peace. You don't."

"They don't deserve peace," she hissed, the moonlight glinting off her fangs. Jarl flinched, but drew his gun. He would protect the other humans. If anything happened to these eight humans, anything at all, then everything was ruined. No human would ever trust the creatures again. Keisha and Jonah would be isolated and hated, as would the new harvesters doing the routes with them. They wouldn't have anyone for those routes and the colony would starve. No, he couldn't let that happen and he leveled the gun at her and tried not to tremble. He was a good shot but hadn't used his gun in over a year. Would he manage to hit her?

"You can't hurt me," she said with a sneer. "It's night. No bullets can hurt me."

That was true, Jarl thought in shock. But how else could he stop her? He thought of the animals he had killed over the past year and what Arlen had taught him. There was a rhythm of life and death on the planet. If his arrow coincided with that rhythm, the animal died. He had learned to persuade the music to let him kill when he needed it. He could never kill more than he needed, but he had learned enough.

Well, he needed to kill her now. He sent his will into the music nearby. If he didn't kill her, everything would be destroyed. Maybe he didn't need to kill her for sustenance, as happened with the animals he killed. But this was just as necessary. Too much would be destroyed if she survived and reached the humans. He felt the music bending towards him. The planet was listening. The planet didn't want to destroy one of her creatures but she was listening.

He poured his heart into the message and her eyes widened as if she suddenly recognized what he was doing.

"You can't turn the planet against me," she said. "How dare you even try!"

He focused on the need to kill her and then, suddenly, a chord ran through him. His finger squeezed on the trigger without his command and it was almost as if he could see the bullet leave the gun and soar through the air. He knew exactly where it would hit even before it struck her in the heart. Blood splattered and she cried out and collapsed backwards.

"That can't kill me," she gasped, but he felt the music of death in his mind. "It can't," she repeated in a frightened voice. "A human can't kill me. Not at night. Not ever. Humans can't do anything."

Jarl took a step closer to her. She was still bleeding and as she coughed, blood ran from the corner of her mouth. When Ender had shot Arlen at night, the bullet had been almost instantly repelled from his body. This bullet had done damage and that damage wasn't vanishing. She went limp and he felt the death around him intensify for a moment, then he felt it replaced by a wave of renewal. He could tell that an animal would be here soon to feast on the body and continue the rhythm of life and death. The creature's death was part of the music of the planet now, and would give rise to new life in the future. He took a deep breath and staggered backwards, the gun falling from his hand.

"Jarl," Arlen said, sounding shocked. "Are you all right?"

"Yeah," he managed.

Arlen bent and scooped up the gun. Jarl took it from him and put the safety back on, then slid it into his belt. He felt numb and couldn't help staring at the body. He had killed someone. Not an accidental killing, either. He had pleaded for it, begged for it, persuaded the planet to allow it. He was a murderer.

"Come on, Jarl," Arlen said, drawing him back towards their home, away from the body and the colony. "You're safe now."

He still felt numb when they reached the cave and Arlen snuggled into the bed with him, holding him tight.

"I killed someone," Jarl finally managed to whisper.

"You had no options," Arlen said softly. "There was nothing else that could have happened. If there was any way to avoid her death, the planet would have done it."

"But I convinced the planet," he said. "I persuaded her. What if I overwhelmed her? What if the creature was right and I've poisoned the planet?"

"You haven't," Arlen said firmly. "But it is true that her music has changed since you joined us. She is learning to adapt to you just as you are adapting to her. Now that there are more humans, your individual influence is lessened and she is learning from others as well, but you will always be special to her. You will always be her first human, and the one closest to her."

"But what if I abused that? What if there was another option that I just didn't see?"

"There wasn't," Arlen said. "If you didn't kill her, I would have."

Jarl shivered. Maybe he would have preferred that. He didn't like to think that he had been the one to shoot her, that it was his bullet to pierce her heart. It would have better for Arlen to kill her. After all, there was a good chance Arlen had killed before. He had never asked Arlen about it and probably never would, but there was a chance Arlen had lured out a human before him and fed on their flesh or nightmares. There was a chance he was already a murderer, and killing the female creature wouldn't be as much of a shock.

"Our planet is in harmony again now," Arlen said softly, stroking his cheek. "Can you feel that? I don't know if you've been able to sense her discontent this past year, the quiet discord in the lower registry of her song, but that creature has been causing disruptions since I first approached you. We exiled her, but perhaps death was the only solution. Now everyone is united behind the idea of helping humans survive. She was the only one who thought otherwise."

"Are you sure? Is it true that creatures can't feed as well? Are you all starving now?"

"Some go hungry," Arlen admitted. "More than before. But there has always been hunger. We eat once a year, sometimes less. Sometimes we grow weak from hunger and die. It is a natural pattern that we have adapted to. We will adapt to this new pattern as well."

So he had killed before. Jarl shivered, but wasn't disgusted at that thought. Arlen needed to survive and he had. He was just grateful Arlen didn't have to feed like that ever again. Jarl would offer all the food he could ever want.

"Once there are more humans, it'll be less of a problem, right?" he asked, and Arlen nodded.

"Someday, each creature will have a human and hunger will vanish. We tolerate the hunger now because we know that day will come. Perhaps not for a hundred years, but it will come."

"I think it'll be sooner," Jarl said.

He thought of the eight people who had come out to the

woods. It wasn't a lot of people but then again, there might be more tomorrow night. When this first batch returned and shared what had happened, surely more would come out tomorrow, and more the next night. He hoped they established their friendships quickly because once they were drawn to the woods, he needed all of them to survive. He wouldn't be allowed to look at the moon when they were drawn out, he already knew. He wouldn't be allowed to influence the outcome. They needed to adapt on their own. And even if it were just these eight, that was nearly tripling the number of people with creatures.

They could start being more open about the creatures being friendly. Next year even more people would come out, perhaps even adults and not just the young people. And eventually, the peace would be seen as a time to greet the creatures and not a brief respite from the horrors of this planet. It was already happening; night was no longer a time of terror. The humans were finally starting to adapt, and in time they would be part of this planet the same way Jarl was.

"Do you feel better?" Arlen asked, stroking his hair back from his forehead.

"I feel hopeful," Jarl said, and Arlen smiled, baring the fangs that Jarl had come to love.

"Is a hopeful mood a good mood for more?" Arlen asked in a teasing voice, his hand stroking down Jarl's back to squeeze his bottom. Jarl chuckled.

"That depends," he said, rolling to straddle Arlen. It was his favorite position now and Arlen enjoyed it immensely as well. "What mood are you in?"

"I'm in the mood for you," he said in a husky voice. "I always am."

"Then I suppose we can do more," Jarl said, leaning forward to peck a kiss on his lips. He no longer missed kissing, since there were so many other ways they were intimate and they could kiss, just not the way Jarl normally thought of as kissing. The fangs prevented a few things, but not many, and Arlen's alien stamina more than made up for it.

Arlen began unwrapping the cloth from Jarl's body, then from his own, and soon Arlen's cock was pressed against his ass as he straddled him. Jarl leaned forward and lifted himself up as Arlen grabbed his cock and angled it into his body. He let out a soft cry as he pressed down on Arlen and felt himself penetrated, then the slow pleasurable slide as he lowered his hips fully. He loved this and he knew Arlen did too from the creature's short breaths and half-closed eyes.

Arlen licked his lips and grabbed Jarl's hips, forcing him to start moving. Jarl was quick to obey, moving on Arlen and feeling in control in a way he never would have imagined, once. He arched his back and felt Arlen strike deep inside him and gasped as pleasure swamped his senses. He was aware of the rhythm of the planet quickening in time with their thrusts. It was no longer as much of a shift after that first time when he was linked to the planet, but the planet was always a part of their lovemaking now and he enjoyed it. It was so much more satisfying than sex with a human ever was.

He rocked his hips and Arlen gasped in sudden pleasure, then Arlen grabbed him and rolled so he was on the bottom with Arlen now pounding inside of him. He let out a breathless laugh. They usually started with Jarl on top but it rarely ended that way and he enjoyed everything about it as Arlen grabbed his leg and adjusted him to get a deeper thrust. He gasped and opened himself to his creature, offering his heart, his body, his everything. Arlen drank deeply from him as they moved together in perfect harmony with the planet and soon a wave of pleasure crashed over Jarl as he cried out and came. Arlen exploded inside him and remained over him, breathing heavily as the music of the planet settled into its usual melody. Jarl was panting and so was Arlen, and then Arlen collapsed beside him and pulled him into an embrace.

"I love you, Jarl," he whispered, and Jarl nuzzled closer.

"I love you, Arlen," he said, meaning the words as he had never meant them with anyone else. This was his home now, here at Arlen's side. Every creature he had met aside from the female creature was friendly to him and with her gone, he felt immeasurably safer. He wouldn't have to be worried about attack or threats or anything from another creature.

The planet still posed dangers, of course. There were still deadly animals that would hunt him if given a chance. But he was safe in a way he never had been before and he was amazed he could feel so safe in the woods that had terrified him his entire life. He remembered the fear that always gripped him the first night of each peace when he worried the night would swallow him and drive him into insanity.

For nearly a decade he had left the colony to harvest the pollen and felt that suffocating fear. He never would have imagined that he could feel safe here, out in the woods at night, especially with a creature next to him. But he was safe, safer than he ever had been before. And soon, other humans would feel this safety. It would take time, but as more and more people adapted, the fear would lessen.

Already people had learned to appreciate the moon; in time they could appreciate the night. It would no longer be a time of terror and nightmares but pleasure and peace. He had made that transition, Keisha and Jonah had, and soon others would follow in their footsteps. It was only a matter of time and humans would be part of this planet that had for so long rejected them.

Once humans learned to love the planet and its creatures, they would become one with it. He wondered if he would be able to feel if Keisha or Jonah had sex with their creatures. Had they felt him just now? Had they felt him every time while they lived in the colony? He hadn't ever considered that. But now that they were part of the planet, everything was wound together. He was an individual, but he was part of a greater whole and unlike with the colony where he resented the greater whole, now he appreciated it. He loved it. He wouldn't want anything else.

Jarl snuggled with Arlen and pulled one of the petals to cover them. For now, he had everything he needed. He was safe and he was with Arlen. And in time, there would be others to join him.

THE END

ABOUT THE AUTHOR

Elizabeth James

Elizabeth James hails from Portland, Oregon and spent many hours of her childhood tucked away in the Gold Room of Powell's Books, reading science fiction and fantasy masterpieces and hidden treasures. She writes romance with strong elements of science fiction and fantasy as a result, focusing on LGBT characters.

THRALL OF DARKNESS

science fiction and fantasy romance publisher

Thrall of Darkness was founded because there is a shortage of good, quality literature featuring gay protagonists that does not reduce gay characters to stereotypes or dismiss them as secondary characters. Every story seeks to challenge the status quo by focusing on gay characters and combining drama, action, and sex into an addicting blend of fun-filled narrative.

You can find more information on Thrall of Darkness novels and short stories at **thrallofdarkness.com.**

BOOKS BY THIS AUTHOR

Demon Season

Taylor just wanted to bond with a regular demon during his first demon season, but instead he ends up with the prince of demons, an incubus! He fights through his fears of intimacy while battling past enemies as he and his demon come to a new understanding.

A Vampire's Desire

Kairos takes a job in an ancient vampire house knowing nothing about them and their society, and immediately falls in love with his boss, a powerful but cold vampire. As he tries to get closer, threats from a rival house threaten to tear them apart.

Tarragon Academy

Tarragon Academy is a college at the foot of a smoldering volcano surrounded in mist and mystery. First-year student Jamie is having a hard time adapting until he meets an upperclassman named Scott. Will Scott help him thrive in his new school, or does Scott have his own reasons for helping the beautiful young freshman?

Dragon Tamer

Luke has heard dragons all his life and when a dragon summons him to raise her dragonlings, he runs away to help her. But the world he enters is fraught with danger and he knows little of the outside world. As the dragons begin dying off and dragon tamers like him become scarce, a rival tribe kidnaps him and everything he knows is thrown into question.

Sagent

Gabriel is a sagent, a sex agent, at the start of his career, but he is already scarred by his previous agency. When he is sent on a dangerous mission to the underbelly of Destiny, everything starts to fall apart. Isolated from his agency and not knowing where to go, Gabriel must choose between returning to safety and Destiny, or staying and forging his own path.

First Prince

Wren is the beautiful yet rebellious first prince of Fontain, forced to move to the Imperial Palace as part of a treaty. Upon arriving, he receives a frigid welcome and realizes his stay will be fraught with danger. When he finds romance in an unexpected place, he realizes that his life may not be as dire as he imagined and pleasure can be found where it is least expected.

Prisoner Of Love

When Prince Tristan is captured in battle, he fully expects to be tortured and killed. But the torture turns to erotic pleasure as he learns that his enemy, Prince Ryan, is in love with him and has been planning his capture with meticulous care for years. Will Tristan hold firm to his principles, or will Ryan's forceful seduction overpower his senses?

Bride Of Albis

Sam and his small crew of space-faring traders have their usual routine permanently shattered when they are kidnapped by pirates. Sam makes a deal with the head of the pirates: he will be sold as a slave in exchange for the freedom of his crew. But when he discovers that the pirate lied and sold his crew as well, he vows vengeance.

Seeking More

Seeking More is a collection of eight contemporary gay romance stories that range from the deeply emotional to action-packed, from hapless MFA students to couples on the brink of a new relationship. Each story is focused not only on steamy romance, of which there is plenty, but also on character development and an emotional connection between reader and character.

Eve Of Etermity

Sabine is a young woman searching for her identity while fleeing the powerful man trying to steal her heart and mind. She's almost under his control when she is kidnapped by a man with conflicting loyalties and a mysterious past who claims to kidnap her in order to rescue her. Will she break free from the men around her?

Treacherous A Dragon's Love

In the middle of the final battle against the great dragon Arostrath, a woman appears bound in golden chains. The King claims her as his reward but the youngest son has an unusual fondness for her that could cast the kingdom into ruin. Will his love for the beautiful and strange woman destroy the kingdom, or does her mystery hide the answer to all of their prayers?

www.ingramcontent.com/pod-product-compliance
Lightning Source LLC
LaVergne TN
LVHW051001080826
845145LV00009B/2402
* 9 7 8 1 9 4 4 9 6 9 1 7 2 *